Danny Dunn and the Automatic House

Jay Williams and
Raymond Abrashkin

Illustrated by Owen Kampen

AN ARCHWAY PAPERBACK
POCKET BOOKS . NEW YORK

I am grateful to John Clare and E. J. Perks for their help in explaining the intricacies of servomechanisms and control systems. I am also indebted to my former Cub Scouts, Leslie Daniels, Jr., and Bill Baker, Jr., for the story and dialogue of Joe's play. The Automatic House was designed by Larry Perron, of Pierre Lutz Associates, Westport, Connecticut.

POCKET BOOKS, a Simon & Schuster division of
GULF & WESTERN CORPORATION
1230 Avenue of the Americas, New York, N.Y. 10020

Copyright © 1965 by Jay Williams and Evelyn Abrashkin

Published by arrangement with McGraw-Hill Book Company
Library of Congress Catalog Card Number: 65-22111

ISBN: 0-671-29977-8

First Pocket Books printing October, 1979

10 9 8 7 6 5 4 3 2 1

Trademarks registered in the United States and other countries.

Printed in the U.S.A.

A Wild Invention!

Danny, Irene and Joe stepped into the bedroom of the automatic house. Irene inspected the bed. "Only sheets, no blankets," she said. "I suppose that's because each room has its own temperature control."

Joe lay down. "Nice," he said. "What's this gimmick here?" He lazily stretched out a hand and turned a small dial in the wall next to the bed.

"It's . . ." Danny began.

Stirring march music began to play. The bed tilted up sharply and Joe went flying to the floor. A closet opened, and a rack shot out bearing a jacket, a pair of trousers and a shirt. "Good morning," said a clear, metallic voice.

". . . an alarm clock," Danny finished.

This book is for
Doug, Andy, and Jim Mantell

Contents

1. "There Are Such Things
   as Robots!"   1

2. The Scuttler   13

3. The Professor's Demonstration   23

4. A Matter of Taste   35

5. Pleasing Mr. String   45

6. The Glazed Look   54

7. Mr. String Is Pleased   64

8. "A Machine for Living"   74

9. Leaving It to Luck   85

10. Emmet Speaks   100

11. The Merry-go-Round   114

12. The Right Key   121

13. A Fair Day   129

1

"There Are Such Things as Robots!"

The leaders of the first American expedition to the Moon were checking over the equipment inside their spaceship before blasting off. Lieutenant Brown held the long sheet of paper, while Captain Karrell called out each item.

"Space suits?"

"Check."

"Fuel?"

"Check."

"Chocolate pie?"

"Hey, wait a minute!" yelled an angry voice. "That's not in the script."

Captain Karrell looked sheepishly at the tall,

dark-haired boy who had jumped out of his seat in the school auditorium.

"I'm sorry, Joe," he said. "It just slipped out. It's what Mom is having for dessert tonight and I've sort of got it on the mind."

"Well, get it off, or I'll give you a lump on the head to go with it." Joe Pearson sank back into his seat, scowling at the stocky boy who played the part of the Captain. "Let's go, now. Do it right. We've only got two more days before the performance."

Danny Dunn, Joe's best friend, grinned at him from the next seat. "Don't be so jumpy," he said, comfortingly. "Everything will be all right on the night."

Joe glared into his friend's freckled face. "And if just one more person says that to me, I'll take off for the Moon myself. And without a rocket!" He groaned. "How do I get myself into these things? Writing and directing the Class Play! It's *your* fault."

"My fault?" Danny ran his fingers through his blazing red hair. "Why, you got *me* involved in it by begging me to take charge of the costumes and props so all the scientific stuff would be right. How is it my fault that you agreed to write and direct the play?"

"Simple. When Miss Arnold asked me if I'd

2

do the job, I asked you whether you could think of any way I could get out of it. And you said you couldn't. So there you are."

Joe sighed and leaned back in his seat, regarding the brightly lighted stage gloomily. "All right, John," he called. "Go ahead. Take it from 'fuel.' "

"And don't fuel around," muttered Danny, with a stifled giggle.

"What?"

"Oh, nothing, nothing."

The pioneers of the expedition continued to check their list, discovered that the oxygen tanks needed refilling, and went offstage to see to it. While they were gone their enemy the sinister Dr. Ziv crept in through the window of the spaceship. Chuckling evilly, he snapped his fingers and behind him clambered a strange figure, a roughly human shape of silvery metal with wires and dials where its face should be and hands which were like the claws of a crab.

"Quick, X-5, before they return, tear loose the wires," rasped Dr. Ziv. "Shatter the control board."

Danny watched and listened in fascination. Although he had seen the play rehearsed for two weeks, he could not help marveling afresh each time at Joe's talent, so unlike his own.

For while Danny knew far more about science than was taught in his grade in school, and could do long division in his head and use a slide rule as easily as he could throw a baseball, the writing of a play was a dark mystery to him. He glanced at Joe in admiration. Just imagine! To think up those ideas, write down all the words for the actors to say, and then to be able to tell them how to speak and move so that the story came to life and worked itself out right in front of your eyes!

The robot on stage finished its job of destruction. Dr. Ziv sent it away and with a laugh of triumph followed it through the window. Brown and Karrell returned and discovered the ruin of their ship's controls.

"Someone doesn't want us to get to the Moon," said Brown.

Karrell, inspecting the control board, shook his head. "No human hand could have done this much damage," he replied. "If I didn't know there were no such things, I'd have said a robot did it."

Danny sat up straight. "Hey, I never heard that line before, Joe," he said. "It's new, isn't it?"

Joe nodded. "I put it in before we started

this afternoon. It seemed to give the situation more zing—more mystery, sort of.''

''But it's all wrong,'' Danny exclaimed.

The actors had been going on with the scene, and Joe flapped his hand impatiently. ''Okay, we'll talk about it later. I want to get through the whole play now so that we can finish the rehearsal by five o'clock.''

The story went on unfolding. The spaceship was repaired; the explorers got to the Moon and found Dr. Ziv there before them; a new radioactive substance was discovered; there was a fearful battle with the robot X-5 ending in the short circuit of his electronic brain, a hand-to-hand combat with Dr. Ziv in the Diamond Caves, and the triumphant return of the pioneers. Joe had a last conference with the actors, settled some final business with the stage manager about curtain calls, warned everyone to be ready for a dress rehearsal in two days, and at last dismissed them. Danny and his assistant, a quiet, efficient boy named Johnny Atwood, packed away all the properties—the Geiger counters, the space tools, the atomic pistols—and hung up the costumes including X-5's metallic carcass, which was made of cardboard boxes covered with aluminum foil. Then he joined his friend, who was sitting in the front row of the auditorium with his head in his hands, moaning softly to himself like a puppy whose owners have gone away forever.

"It'll never be ready," he said to Danny. "Never! They still don't know all their lines, and that dope Willy acts the part of the Chief of the Space Program as if he was afraid his head was going to come unglued and fall off!"

Danny patted his back. "Joe, it'll be all—"

"Don't say it! Don't say it!"

"Okay. But you know you're always looking on the gloomy side of things. It's an exciting show and it looks great. The only thing I think you ought to change is that one new line."

"What line?"

"About there being no such things as robots. Because there are. Lots of them."

Joe slowly went, "tk, tk, tk," with a sympathetic look at his friend. "Too much thinking," he said. "I always knew that giant brain would snap one of these days under the strain."

"Don't be a nut," Danny grinned.

"But look, Dan, now you're seeing robots

everywhere, crawling all over the place, clanging and rattling—"

"Oh, poop! What do you think a robot is, anyway?" Danny demanded.

Joe looked around the auditorium as if he expected to spot one lurking somewhere. "Why—why—everybody knows what they are," he replied. "They're machines that look like men. Alive but not alive. They stalk around—like this!" He jumped up and stood stiff and straight, his hands formed into claws. "Like X-5. They walk, clank, clank, and their machinery goes *doing! peep! doing! peep!*" He rolled his eyes, twisted up his mouth, and clutched at the air. Then he blew out a long breath, and subsided. "Oh, for gosh sakes, Dan, *you* know."

Danny was rolling in his seat, snorting and gurgling with laughter. "I don't know whether you're Frankenstein's monster or a teenage werewolf," he managed to say. "But it was a neat performance. Anyway, you're all wrong."

He pulled himself together. "Joe, I could make a telephone that looked like a person, but it wouldn't be a robot. I could fix up a thing that would clank around and go cross-eyed like

7

you just did, but it wouldn't be a robot, either. A robot is a machine, all right, but there's got to be something that makes it different from other machines.''

''It talks?'' Joe suggested.

''No. A tape recorder talks.''

''Oh, well, I mean it just doesn't repeat words you put into it. It—it—well, I guess it would be a machine that understood what you said, a machine that thinks.''

''All right. Or put it this way—it would follow directions, obey instructions, and make choices. It's a machine you can give instructions to, and it follows them and chooses the right thing to do at the right time. So you could have simple robots that follow simple instructions, sort of like ordinary workmen. Then you could have more complicated robots that figure things out for themselves and make complicated choices. The complicated ones would learn, and be able to reason.''

''Mph!'' Joe grunted skeptically. ''You can't tell me machines like that are all around us.''

''Oh, well, no, maybe not. But look, there's one of those simple robots right there on the wall.''

''Where?'' Joe jumped up and whirled around.

Danny tapped him on the arm. "I'll show you."

He led his friend to the big double doors at the back of the hall. There was a small round dial and a thermometer set in the wall next to them.

"That's a thermostat," Joe said.

"Right the first time. Now, we tell this little machine that we want it to keep the temperature in the hall at 65 degrees. Okay. When the temperature drops below that, the workman-machine turns on the furnace. Right? And as soon as the temperature is up to 65, the robot shuts off the furnace."

Joe rubbed his nose. "I see your point," he said. "But you can't tell me that a thermostat really thinks."

"No, of course not. It just does one simple job. Yes, no. On, off. Bang-bang. That's what engineers call it: a bang-bang system. But you put lots of these bang-bangs together, and give them a lot of information to refer to, and you've got a kind of computer. And that's a machine that can put two and two together and come up with the right answers. A kind of robot."

Joe shook his head vigorously. "I don't care," he said. "That's not what *I* call a robot.

9

You show me something that goes creeping around, going *doing! peep! doing! peep!* and figuring things out for itself, and maybe I'll believe you."

Danny set his jaw stubbornly. "Okay," he said. *"O*-kay. I wasn't supposed to talk about this, but you're my best friend and I'll show you. Professor Bullfinch has been working on something. You come on home with me, and you can see it for yourself."

Danny's mother was housekeeper for a noted scientist, Professor Euclid Bullfinch. The Professor was a member of the faculty of Midston University, but his discoveries and inventions had brought him some fame and enough money so that he could maintain his own small private laboratory and conduct his own researches. Mr. Dunn had died when Danny was only a baby, and the Professor had taken a great liking to the child, treating him like a son and teaching him a great deal about science.

The house on Elm Street was a sprawling, old-fashioned place, full of unexpected corners and added to by its many owners over the years. It had been built in 1750 for a gentleman named Jonathan Turner, who had been a friend of Benjamin Franklin's and had experimented with the new "electrical fluid." A hundred years later, a wing had been added for Mr. Turner's great-great-nephew, who had been interested in the new science of photography; thirty years after, his son had put a cupola on the roof from which he could examine the stars through a homemade telescope. "The old house is used to inquisitive people and knows how to make them comfortable," Professor Bullfinch remarked with a chuckle. "The least we can do is give it something in return." He himself had built a long, one-story addition in the back, one room of which served as a laboratory, the other as a library and storage room for records and files.

It was to the laboratory that Danny led Joe. Although it could be reached by a private entrance outside in the rear, Dan went through the house so that he could leave his school books on the hall table. A corridor led to the back of the house, and after calling a greeting to his mother, Danny took Joe along this to the lab door.

"Now," he said, as he softly turned the knob of the door, "let me handle this. Professor Bullfinch may be busy, but I think I can talk him into letting you see his new work.

11

You'll be surprised, Joe. You've never seen anything like it.''

He cautiously opened the door. Then he froze. Behind him, Joe gave a gulp of alarm.

There, almost face to face with them, gazing out of round blank eyes, stood a strange, unearthly shape.

2
The Scuttler

The creature was less than three feet high. It seemed to have no hands or legs; at the top was a round head covered by a brown knitted cap, and below that was a shapeless white woolen garment that dropped in folds to the floor. Its face was without expression. There was a blob of a nose, a small mouth, and enormous round blue eyes. The thing stood silent and motionless as the two boys stared at it.

At last Joe whispered, "Is that it? Is that what you wanted to show me?"

Danny shook his head. "I don't know what it is," he whispered back. "I've never seen it before."

"Do you think it's alive?"

"I don't know."

"Hm," said Joe. "Then why are we whispering?"

Danny wasn't listening. With his hands on his knees, he peered more closely at the odd little being. "It doesn't seem to be breathing," he said. "But look, its eyes move to follow us when we move."

Joe tiptoed to one side. Then, without warning, he suddenly shouted, "BOO!"

Not a muscle quivered. The creature remained as motionless as before. Only its mouth opened, wider than seemed possible. Danny involuntarily jerked back, and Joe clapped his hands over his ears. But not a sound came out. The mouth closed again.

"It's a Martian," Joe said, backing away. "I always knew this was going to happen some day. They've invaded Earth at last. They probably have a spaceship in the backyard, and they've come here because Professor Bullfinch is so famous that they wanted to capture him, and any minute now they'll come screebling out of the walls and grab us."

"Screebling?" Danny said.

"What else would Martians do?" said Joe.

"I'm not sure," Danny replied. "But I'll tell you something. This Martian's nose is running."

Joe eyed it. "You're right. So?"

"So I don't think it's a Martian."

"Couldn't it be a Martian with a cold?" Joe was beginning, but at that moment, a fearful racket broke out. First one, then a second, then a third dog began barking wildly just outside the open windows of the laboratory.

A girl in blue jeans and a checked shirt came running out of the records room into the laboratory, her brown braids flying. She leaned out of a window and shouted, "Scat! Go home!" Then she whirled and pointed an accusing finger at the little Martian. "Emmet!" she cried. "You've been screaming again."

"Hi, Irene," Danny said. "Is this thing yours?"

The girl smiled. She was Danny's next-door neighbor. Her father, Dr. Miller, was a colleague of Professor Bullfinch's, and taught astronomy at Midston University.

"You might say that," she answered. "He's my cousin, Emmet. I'm supposed to be looking after him, but he's an awful nuisance. This screaming he does—"

"What screaming?" said Joe. "He didn't make a sound."

"He can scream in a pitch above ordinary sound," Irene explained. "Nobody but dogs can hear him. It drives them crazy. Whenever he feels threatened, he does it and all the dogs in the neighborhood come running, barking their heads off. Now you quit it, do you hear, Emmet?" she added, severely. "These are friends of mine. If you don't behave, I'll tell Uncle George and he'll take your submarine sweater away."

"Gnop," said Emmet sulkily.

Danny eyed the long white garment that clothed Emmet. "Is that his submarine sweater?" he asked.

"Yes. My Uncle George—his father—wore it during the war. Emmet loves it; he thinks it makes him look military."

"Mnuz," Emmet said, proudly.

"That's an interesting language he talks," Joe said. "Is that from the war, too?"

"Don't be silly, Joe. It's perfectly clear. He just said, 'It does too make me look military,' " Irene replied.

Joe nodded. "Uh-huh," he said. "It was clear as anything." He stretched out a cautious finger and touched Emmet on the cheek. "You're sure he *is* alive?" he said. "He looks like one of those wind-up toys."

A beaming smile split Emmet's face, as he gazed up at Joe. With great labor, he got his hands out of the sweater sleeves, and with one finger touched Joe in return.

"Oog," he said.

"Ugh?" said Joe. "Why am I ugh?"

"He said, 'Good,' " Irene translated. "He likes you. That's his word for hot fudge sundaes."

"Why, Joe, how sweet you are," Danny grinned.

"Never mind that," growled Joe. "Didn't you want to show me the Professor's new invention? Never mind this horrible kid. Let's get back to business."

"Yes, where is Professor Bullfinch, Irene?" Danny asked.

"In the records room, talking to Daddy and Uncle George."

Danny led the way through the laboratory. The records room, not very spacious to begin with, today seemed unbelievably crowded. Dr. Miller, a worried-looking man, sat in the swivel chair at the desk, leaning far back at the risk of falling over on his head. Uncle George, who was as tall and massive as a football player, leaned on the filing cabinet. Professor Bullfinch himself perched on the edge of the desk with his back against the bookcase. The Professor was in his shirt sleeves, his hands clasped around one knee, and he somehow managed to look comfortable although his position was so precarious. His eyes twinkled behind their thick-rimmed spectacles, and his old pipe, clenched between his teeth, sent up such a cloud of smoke that his bald head seemed to be on fire.

"I'm not exaggerating, I tell you," Dr. Miller was saying. "That man is going to turn Midston University upside down."

"I'm sure it's not as bad as that," said the Professor. "He may raise some dust, but I don't think he's going to shake us up too much."

Danny and Joe listened, open-mouthed. The Professor caught sight of them at the door and nodded with a smile.

"Hullo, Dan. Hi, Joe," he said. "I'm afraid I can't ask you to come in—the room's too full."

"Gosh!" said Danny. "Who is the man you're talking about? He sounds like a giant. Pick up the University and shake it—?"

"Oh, he's far from a giant," said the Professor. "A perfectly ordinary fellow."

"He's stronger than you think," grunted Dr. Miller.

"I don't get it," said Danny. "Perfectly ordinary and strong enough to pick up a building?"

"Don't let them kid you," put in Uncle George. "They're talking about Mr. String, one of the trustees of Midston University. He has some ideas which they think may make some disagreeable changes in the old place. Here—who's that I see peeking around your knee? Not my old friend Submarine Sam?"

Emmet pushed past Danny and ran to his father, who swung him up into the air with a deep laugh. "How are things, skipper?" said Uncle George.

"Oog," Emmet said, earnestly. "Ipy emma boz."

"Very interesting," said Uncle George. "Irene, please translate."

"He just says he met these two boys— Danny and Joe—and they are very nice," Irene replied.

"Good thing I've got an intelligent niece," said Uncle George. "Don't know how I manage in New York without her."

"It's astonishing how she understands him," Irene's father said, shaking his head. "Don't you think, George, it's time Emmet learned to talk? After all, he's three years old."

"He'll talk when he's ready," Uncle George grinned. "I think he's figured out that talking only means trouble, like 'Wash behind your ears,' or 'Make your bed.' Pretty smart of him. As long as he can't talk he doesn't have to do any schoolwork."

"But actually he *is* talking," said Professor Bullfinch. "And very well, too. Only not in English. He is using a private code, something like the way men talk to computers."

"Is that how you talk to the machine you've been working on?" Uncle George asked.

"Ah, my machine." Professor Bullfinch jumped up. He thrust his pipe in his pocket and rubbed his hands. "We've wandered from the subject, haven't we? That's what I invited you over to see. Let's go into the laboratory."

Danny glanced at Joe with a wink, but said nothing. Since the invitation obviously included the children, they all followed the Professor and the other two men into the next room.

Long and wide as it was, the laboratory seemed almost as cramped and cluttered as the records room. Every type and variety of scientific equipment stood on shelves or in cupboards, or lay strewn about on the stone-topped lab benches. In one corner, a space had been cleared between a portable welding torch, a 4-inch reflector telescope, and a large electromagnet. In the middle of this space stood a gray metal cabinet about as high as Emmet. It rested on four small rubber-tired wheels. Near the top of each of its sides were two round openings, like eyes. There was nothing else.

"There you are," said the Professor, waving a hand proudly. "An auto-instructional, multi-choice, mobile tracker using metachromic dye switches for its memory banks and employing both linear and nonlinear servomechanisms."

"That's a mouthful," said Dr. Miller.

"Quite so," the Professor agreed. "I prefer to call it a Scuttler."

"A *Scuttler?*" Danny said. "Why do you call it that? What does it do?"

Professor Bullfinch laid a finger alongside his nose.

"It scuttles," he said, mysteriously.

3
The Professor's Demonstration

There was a long silence. Everyone looked at everyone else.

Then Irene said, "You mean that it—it scuttles? Around? From one place to another?"

"Exactly," said Professor Bullfinch.

"Oh," said Irene. "Ah. I see."

The Professor laughed. "Evidently you don't see. I know it sounds very peculiar. Perhaps I'd better demonstrate how it works."

He picked up a small box which looked as though it had a microphone built into it, and walked to the other end of the laboratory. "Now I'd like you to notice, please," he said, "that between the Scuttler and me there are lab benches, pieces of apparatus, stools, and all sorts of other things. All right?" He raised the microphone to his lips. "Come here, Scuttler," he said. "Now. Go!"

The metal cabinet began to buzz softly. Rolling smoothly on its rubber wheels, it moved out of the corner. It neatly avoided the telescope, dodged around one end of a stone-topped laboratory bench, and came towards the Professor. It moved in a series of swift, short rushes. When it came to an obstacle, such as a stool, it did not turn but darted to one side and then forward again. It became clear why the Professor called it a Scuttler, for there was something crablike, or insectlike, about the way it moved. It rolled up to the Professor and stopped.

"Part One of the demonstration," said the Professor, taking off his glasses and wiping them on his necktie.

Dr. Miller was the first to speak. "Splendid!" he cried. "It homed in on the signal like a pigeon."

"I'm only a simple-minded architect," said Uncle George. "I don't understand it. How did you get the thing to do that?"

"That part of it is fairly easy," the Professor

replied. "The word *Now* started a radio signal operating from the control box, this thing that looks like a cross between a portable radio and a microphone. The Scuttler's built-in antenna picked up the signal and the machine began to move towards it. Now, as long as the signal grows stronger the machine knows that it is on the right track. If the signal grows weaker, then a series of servomechanisms inside the Scuttler correct its position, and keep it going in the right direction."

"Why doesn't it bump into the furniture?" asked Uncle George.

"Radar," answered the Professor. "A modified radar device tells the Scuttler when there's something in its path and the servomechanisms guide it around the obstacle."

"You keep saying 'servomechanisms,' " said Irene. "I've heard the word but I don't know what it means."

"Hmm." Professor Bullfinch rubbed his forehead. "Let's call them something else. Servos are one kind of automatic control system. They operate by feedback."

"Feedbag?" said Joe. "That's something I can understand."

"No, no, control your appetite, Joe," chuckled the Professor. "Feed*back*. Means just what it says. Look here—you reach out to pick up a pencil. Your eyes feed back information about where the pencil is, so that your brain can make corrections in the hand which is reaching out. That way, you reach out the right distance and to the right spot so that you can find the pencil. Well, we can arrange the same sort of thing in a machine in a number of different ways.''

"So people have servomechanisms in them?'' asked Danny.

"Oh, yes. Lots and lots of them.''

Joe shivered. "Gives me the creeps,'' he said. "It makes you feel you're full of switches and cogwheels and gears.''

"It's not quite that bad, Joe,'' said the Professor. "But if you think of your nerves as wires connected to millions and millions of tiny switches. . . .''

"You're just making it worse,'' Joe groaned.

"I'm sorry,'' said Professor Bullfinch, sympathetically. "In any case, there are all sorts of error-finding and error-correcting systems. The Scuttler follows the signal, which is the information about direction being fed into it. The servos inside the Scuttler read that information and make corrections for mistakes. The radar beam gives it information about whether there's anything in its way, and other servos make corrections for *that,* and steer it away from the obstacles. Is that clear?''

"It's like what an antimissile missile does, isn't it?'' said Danny. "It homes on a missile, and I suppose servos inside it keep it on course.''

"That's right. Now we'll go on to the second part of my demonstration. And for this, Dan, I'd like your help.''

"What do you want me to do, Professor?''

"I want you to race the Scuttler.''

"Race it? You mean, like a hundred-yard dash?''

"No. More like a steeplechase, or an obstacle race. You'll both start here and race to that far corner.'' Professor Bullfinch pointed to a spot between the outside door of the laboratory and the last of the row of windows. "There are two lab benches, some stools, a wooden crate, a case of glass flasks, and a microscope stand between here and there. The only rule is that you mustn't climb over anything. All right?''

"Okay. Are you going to the corner to send a signal to the Scuttler?''

"Oh, no. That's the whole point of the demonstration. I'll tell it where to go, just as I've told you. Then you'll both start even, when I say *Go*. All set?"

Danny nodded.

"Great guns!" said Joe. "You ought to be able to beat a tin box."

The Professor spoke into the control microphone. "Sector Four," he said. "Ready . . . steady . . . Go!"

On the word, Danny was off. He had already chosen his course, marking out by eye the quickest way to go. The space was narrow and he had to be alert; nimbly he pivoted on his toes around the ends of benches, swooped around the wooden crate and almost lost his balance, recovered, and shot past the case of flasks and the microscope stand. But fast as he was, the Scuttler was even faster. It had chosen a different route and went zigzagging along as if it had gone crazy. It arrived in the corner an instant before Danny got there.

"Whew!" Danny panted. "That thing— sure covers—the ground!"

Irene, staring in amazement, said, "But how did it do it? I can understand how it followed your signal before. But this time there was no signal at all. Or did you have something hidden in the corner?"

"Ready . . . steady . . . Go!"

Uncle George ran a large, freckled hand over his hair. "You told it to go to Sector Four, Bullfinch," he said. "You must have had the route planned ahead of time. Is that it?"

"Not at all," said the smiling Professor, clearly very pleased at the success of his machine. "The Scuttler did exactly what Danny did. It looked at the problem of getting from one spot to another, computed the quickest way, and went."

"Yes, but what was that Sector Four stuff?" Joe demanded.

"Ah, well, you see," said the Professor, "I have to be able to talk machine talk so that the Scuttler will understand me. The word *Now,* which starts the radio signal, also means come to the place where the control box is. *Go* starts the Scuttler moving. But when I want to send it somewhere else—somewhere where there's no radio signal to call it—I need to give it directions. So I set up a code for this room, or for any part of this house. Now the laboratory is 12 feet wide by 21 feet long, so I divided it into 3-foot squares, gave each a number, and put that grid into the Scuttler's computer system. Something like a road map, you might say. Sector Four is my code way of telling the Scuttler to go to that particular corner."

"Not a bad idea for me," said Uncle George. "I ought to set up a code like that so that I can understand Emmet." He glanced around. "Where *is* Emmet, by the way?"

"He's here," Joe said, jerking a thumb behind him. Emmet was standing as close to Joe as he could get, looking up at him with round, admiring eyes. "He's been crowding me ever since the demonstration started. I think he's afraid the Scuttler will get him if he doesn't watch out."

"Well, you remember he said you were *oog,* Joe," Irene giggled.

Emmet crooked his finger at Joe.

"What's he want now?" Joe asked.

"He wants you to lean over towards him," said Irene. "He probably wants to tell you something."

Joe bent over. When his face was close to Emmet's, the little one stuck out a long pink tongue and licked Joe's nose.

"Hey!" Joe jumped back with a disgusted look.

"Apy," said Emmet, with satisfaction.

Uncle George uttered his booming laugh. "I know that word," he said. "He's saying that you're tasty, Joe. He always likes to taste his friends. It's a great compliment. Most of the time he makes awful faces at the way people taste."

"I can live without such wet compliments," Joe growled. "Go on, you little pest, go to your father and lick *his* nose."

But Danny, who knew Joe better than anyone else did, knew that his friend was flattered. He could see that Joe was trying not to smile.

Dr. Miller had been studying the Scuttler with his chin in his hand. Now he said, "Bullfinch, I think this might do it!"

Professor Bullfinch raised his eyebrows. "Do what?"

"Solve our String problem. It might be just what he's looking for."

Uncle George scooped up Emmet and held him firmly, although he wriggled like a kitten and tried to get down. "At ease, Skipper," said Uncle George, and to Dr. Miller he added, "You mean what he's looking for for the fair, don't you?"

"Exactly. The Scuttler would make a most interesting display."

"What fair, Professor," asked Danny. "And what's a string problem?"

Professor Bullfinch pulled out his pipe with a chuckle, and tamped down the tobacco with a broad thumb. "Dr. Miller is not being very respectful about Mr. String, I'm afraid. You see, Mr. String has recently become a member of the board of trustees. He is quite rich and influential, and is full of ideas about increasing the University's prestige. Dr. Richards, our good president, is a patient man and doesn't want to have any trouble. In any case, he can't really object since Mr. String simply insists that we ought to do more to make the public understand what a university contributes to the community. It's not a bad idea, you know.''

"Hmph!" grunted Dr. Miller. "It's the way he puts it that I object to. He says he doesn't want people to think we're a bunch of long-haired dreamers. 'Live-wire public relations is what we need,' he said."

"Well, yes, but that's just his way of talking," said the Professor soothingly. "In any case, Danny, there's an important Science and Industry Fair planned for this summer, and Midston has been chosen as the site for it. Mr. String is hoping that the big open meadow on the other side of the University will be used, and he is particularly anxious for us to put on a display which will—er—"

"Knock their eye out," put in Dr. Miller. "That was the way he put it, if I remember right."

"Just so." Professor Bullfinch regarded the Scuttler thoughtfully. "And you think this might please him?"

"Oh, yes, Professor," Danny said. "Dr. Miller's right. Nothing could be better. Why don't you invite Mr. String here to see it?"

The Professor nodded slowly. "Well, if you all feel that strongly," he said, "I think we might give it a try."

4
A Matter
of Taste

With his elbows on the kitchen table, and his face firmly wedged between his hands, Danny watched his mother at work. Efficiently and smoothly, with a minimum of effort, she moved about the room, glancing into a pot on the stove and adding a dash of something, chopping this, beating that, mixing both. It was, he thought dreamily, something like the orderly bustle he had once seen in a large chemical laboratory. My mother, he mused, is a kind of research scientist of dinners.

Abruptly, he said, "Mom, how would you go about getting rid of a kid?"

Mrs. Dunn brushed a drooping lock of red hair out of her eyes with the back of her hand. "Some sort of mystery story idea, Dan?" she said, absently—she was wondering whether a bit more dill in the pot roast might be an interesting idea. "You mean, who committed the murder, Inspector Maigret?"

"No, I mean suppose some kid is pestering somebody. How would you get rid of him?"

Mrs. Dunn bent a sharp eye on her son. "Is this a real question or a theoretical one? Do you mean, how would I, for example, keep you from pestering me while I'm trying to cook?"

"Am I pestering you? Gee, I'm sorry," Danny said. "I kind of enjoy watching you. It's like watching Professor Bullfinch prepare an experiment."

Mrs. Dunn smiled, and tapped Dan lightly on the head with her wooden spoon. "I'm just joking, dear. I love having you here. But seriously, what *are* you talking about?"

"Well, it's Emmet. Every time Joe comes over here, Emmet pops up from somewhere and hangs around him. I mean, he's a nice little boy and all that but he's getting to be a nuisance."

"Dear me," said Mrs. Dunn. "I didn't realize Joe was such a Pied Piper. What's his attraction? Does he tell fine stories, or play games?"

Danny shook his head. "Emmet says he tastes good."

Mrs. Dunn broke into delighted laughter. "Lovely," she cried. "I must try a taste of him myself, one of these days." Then she grew serious, thoughtfully nibbling the end of the spoon. "Well," she said, "I suggest that you try to change Joe's taste. And if that doesn't work—I suppose the best thing he can do is keep out of sight for a while. After all, the

Millers are only staying with Irene's parents for a few more days.''

"Change his taste . . . !" Danny jumped to his feet. "Thanks, Mom. I knew I could depend on you."

He went to the shelf where Mrs. Dunn kept her spices. With wrinkled brow, he looked over the array of little boxes and bottles. "Allspice," he murmured. "That sounds too good. So do nutmeg and cinnamon. Ginger—no, it might make him taste like gingerale. Ah, pepper! That should do it."

"Now, Danny," his mother warned, from her post at the stove, "don't get carried away. You're always jumping into things without thinking them through—"

But he was gone, stuffing the can of pepper into his back pocket.

He ran out into the backyard, where Joe was to meet him to discuss the next day's dress rehearsal of the play. It was difficult for Danny to do nothing for more than a minute or two at a stretch, and so, to pass the time, he began planning an irrigation project which would involve damming up the stream near the woods, bringing the water in a channel to the vegetable garden, and then piping it by an overhead aqueduct to his mother's roses. Just as he was drawing the design for the aqueduct on a piece of board, he was interrupted by Professor Bullfinch.

"Danny!" The Professor leaned out of one of the windows of the laboratory. "Can you recall where I put the control box for the Scuttler?"

Danny thought for a moment. "Didn't you put it on the long stone-topped bench the other day, when you were demonstrating it to us?" he asked.

"I thought so, but now I can't find it," replied the Professor.

Danny ran into the laboratory. The bench in question was covered with odds and ends of apparatus, but after searching for a moment among the tubes and switches and coils of wire, Danny emerged with the control box. "No wonder you couldn't find it," he said. "Things get buried quickly in here."

"Ah—er—yes," the Professor said. "I was working on an interesting little sideline this morning, and somehow matters must have got out of hand."

He took the box and went to the inner door. "By the way," he said, "when you leave the lab, don't close this door. Be sure to leave it wide open. Better shut that window so that the wind doesn't accidentally slam the door.''

''All right, Professor,'' Danny said, a little surprised. ''But why?''

The Professor, however, had hurried out into the corridor.

Danny went to shut the window. Joe was on the lawn, peering rather anxiously about.

''Hi,'' called Danny. ''Here I am.''

''Have you seen Emmet?'' Joe said, in a loud whisper.

''No, but come on in. You'll be safe here.''

''Safe! Ha! For a minute, maybe.'' Joe darted through the back door and dramatically fell against the wall. ''I feel like a hunted man—Daredevil Joe Trailed by the Pint-sized Monster from Outer Space.''

''I think I have the solution to your problem,'' Danny said, with a wink.

''Really? What are you going to do—have Emmet kidnapped?''

''Now, Joe. You know you really like the kid,'' Danny chuckled. ''I've watched your face when he's around. You pretend to be annoyed, but I can see you grinning.''

''It's a grin of anguish,'' Joe replied. ''No, seriously, he *is* a funny little guy, sort of like a pet kitten. I don't mind him following me. It's the nose-licking I can't stand. My good gosh, how would *you* like to be a human ice cream cone?''

At that moment, Irene entered the lab. ''Is this a top-level meeting or is the public invited?'' she said. ''And who is that perfectly blug man with Professor Bullfinch?''

''Blug? What's blug?'' asked Danny.

''It's Emmet's word for something like spinach, or milk of magnesia. Between ugly and blah, I guess.''

''Where'd you see this blug fellow?'' said Joe.

''When I came through the front hall, he and the Professor were sitting in the living room. I said hello, and Professor Bullfinch said hello, but this man just glared at me.''

''I don't know who it is,'' said Danny. ''Maybe a salesman, and maybe he's feeling sour because the Professor won't buy whatever he's selling.''

''And where is our charming little playmate today?'' Joe asked, with elaborate courtesy.

''Oh, don't worry. I left Emmet playing with the insides of a percolator.''

''You did, eh?'' said Joe. He glanced away from Irene and out the window. ''Think again.

He has passed up the pleasures of percolator research. How does that kid find me? He's a kind of boy bloodhound."

The outside door rattled. Slowly the knob turned; the door opened a little way, and Emmet's round face appeared.

"O?" he said. This was Emmet-code for "Joe."

"The Snark is a Boojum!" Joe exclaimed. "I shall softly and suddenly vanish away."

"No you won't," said Danny. "Come here, quick! I'll fix things."

He snatched the pepper out of his pocket. He slid back the top and shook the box in Joe's face. He had intended to sprinkle only a little on his friend's nose, but haste and excitement ruined the plan. The top of the box flew off. A cloud of pepper filled the air.

For one terrible minute, the laboratory was a bedlam of sneezes.

"Danny! What—ka-chow!—did you—ka-CHOW!" gasped Irene.

"*Chew!* A-a-help!—atCHEW!" wheezed Joe.

Danny's face was purple, and Emmet, holding onto Irene to keep from flying backward, sneezed and wept alternately.

Joe, who had received the largest dose, staggered away blindly. Still sneezing, he fell over a stool and sprawled across the top of one of the lab tables. A bottle went crashing to the floor and the liquid which spilled began sending up white fumes, like wisps of smoke.

"Oooh-*choo!* Now look what you—choo!" cried Danny.

He ran to the window and threw it wide open.

"Sulphuric a-*chew*-cid!" he said. "Get Emmet up off the floor, Irene. Don't step in it! I'll get something to neutralize it."

Irene lifted Emmet and put him firmly on top of the nearest flat surface—the cabinet of the Scuttler.

"You stay there," she said, sharply. "Don't move. Dangerous!"

"Ka-bzz!" sneezed Emmet, piteously.

Danny had gone to one of the cupboards. He took down a large box of baking soda which the Professor kept for just such emergencies. He ripped open the lid and carefully poured the powder over the pool of acid. There was a great frothing and foaming as the dangerous stuff was neutralized by the alkaline soda and made harmless.

"We'll need some sawdust and a broom," said Danny. He turned. He stood gaping for a moment, and then shouted, "Hey! Wait!"

The Scuttler was moving. Deftly avoiding Irene, and skirting the edge of the lab bench with a smooth movement, it darted to the open inner door. Before any of the three young people could move, it had vanished into the corridor, bearing with it the round-eyed Emmet, too startled to make a sound.

5
Pleasing
Mr. String

Professor Bullfinch had been having an uncomfortable quarter of an hour. He always found it hard to think ill of anyone, and usually did his best to be agreeable in any sort of company, but he had to admit that his guest was a difficult person to get along with.

Mr. Wilbur String looked nothing like his name. His fat face blazed with little red blood vessels, and was constantly moist with perspiration. He was large and rather pear shaped. As a fat man, he should by rights have been slow moving and jolly, but as if determined to be contrary he was energetic and snappish.

"We'll have to get after the town and make them fix the road out in front of this house, Bullfinch," he said, when he came in. "It's full of holes, and I have a new car. So this is your place, is it? One of those old houses, eh? High time they tore these old places down and put up some clean modern houses around the University."

The Professor offered him an armchair. "I never sit in them," growled Mr. String. "My father was stuck in a Windsor armchair once, and they had to saw the arms off."

"Would you like some tea?" asked the Professor.

"Never touch it. It's full of tannin—the stuff they use to tan leather. You can imagine what it does to the stomach. You ought to know all this, being a scientist."

He plumped himself on the sofa, which groaned under his weight. "Well, let's get to business," he said. "I've got six other meetings to attend today. Where's this revolutionary new robot of yours?"

"It's not exactly a robot, Mr. String," the Professor said, mildly. "I told you over the phone that it was a robotlike machine, employing feedback control systems and radar—"

46

"I don't see the difference," said Mr. String. "Never mind. Go on."

"Well, the idea is based on certain experiments made by W. Grey Walter, in England, with a machine capable of learning—"

"Ha! So in the first place it isn't an original invention, is that it?" cried Mr. String.

"My dear sir," said the Professor, beginning to feel annoyed, "I don't know what you mean by an 'original invention.' All scientists draw upon the work of others. In any case, I am not in the inventing business. The Scuttler is not an invention, it's a machine for experimenting with and demonstrating certain control operations."

Mr. String grunted. "Very interesting. Well, bring it out. Let's see it."

The Professor picked up the Scuttler's control box. "I'll do better than that," he said. "I'll call it, and it will bring itself out."

Mr. String raised his eyebrows at that, but said nothing. Professor Bullfinch spoke into the control microphone.

"Now," he said, thus activating the radio signal. "Go."

He put down the box and waited expectantly, looking at the open door of the living room. Mr. String could not help sitting up straight, impressed in spite of himself. A whirring was heard in the hall. Into the room shot the Scuttler. And on top of it was Emmet, sitting still as he had been ordered. Swathed in his father's huge, white submarine sweater, with his small feet sticking out at one end and his round head

at the other, he was an even more surprising sight than the Scuttler itself.

The Scuttler came to a stop, directly in front of Mr. String.

Mr. String stared up at Emmet. Emmet stared down at Mr. String.

"It's alive!" Mr. String exclaimed.

Emmet's eyes filled with terror at the harsh, sudden noise. His mouth opened wide.

Danny burst into the room, with Joe and Irene at his heels.

"No, Emmet!" he yelled. "Don't do it."

It was too late. From outside came the distant yapping and baying of the neighborhood dogs.

Irene rushed to the Scuttler and grabbed at Emmet to shut him up. Her hands missed their hold. Emmet shot neatly off the smooth top of the machine and landed in Mr. String's lap.

Mr. String gave an undignified quack, tried to stand up, and only succeeded in snarling himself in Emmet's sweater. He flopped back on the sofa. Emmet reached up, took hold of Mr. String's ears to steady himself, and delicately licked the tip of his nose.

"Blug!" said Emmet, making a wry face.

Irene snatched him up. "Oh, poor Emmet,"

she crooned. "Poor baby. Did he have a terrible ride?"

Emmet smiled angelically, lying back in her arms like an enormous, overstuffed teddy bear.

"What—what—what is the meaning of this?" shouted Mr. String, furiously scrubbing the end of his nose with his handkerchief.

"It was an accident," Danny said. "Gee, I'm sorry, sir. If I hadn't tried to pour the pepper on Joe's nose—and then the sulphuric acid spilled—"

"Sulphuric? Pepper?" Mr. String struggled to get to his feet. "Is this a madhouse? What's going on, Bullfinch?"

Professor Bullfinch's face was a study. He was trying not to laugh, but at the same time he couldn't help being upset. He passed a hand over his eyes once or twice, and at last said, "I'm sure there's a perfectly rational explanation. If everyone will please be quiet. . . . Joe, perhaps you wouldn't mind stepping outside and shooing away those dogs. I can hardly hear myself think. Irene, you'd better take Emmet into the kitchen and revive him with a glass of milk or something."

When they had gone, the Professor turned to Danny. "Well, Dan?" he said.

Danny explained what had happened. "So

you see," he finished, "we didn't know you were going to operate the Scuttler or we never would have put Emmet on top of it."

"Perfectly irresponsible," fumed Mr. String. "You allow children to fool around in your laboratory, Professor?"

"But we weren't. . . ."

"That'll do, Dan," said the Professor, quietly. "I wouldn't say that the children fool around in the laboratory, Mr. String."

"Mr. *String!*" Danny gulped, and was silent with horror.

The Professor went on, "Danny has the run of the lab simply because he is generally responsible, and knows a good deal about science. He hopes to become a scientist himself, one day. Irene is also planning to become a physicist when she grows up. They don't usually get into such messes. But in any case, I feel that the interest of children should be encouraged. They will be the men and women of the future. Surely you must realize how important it is to open the doors to them for research, for speculation, or the free play of their imagination?"

"A university is not a playground for grammar school children," replied Mr. String harshly. "I'm afraid, Professor, that I cannot go along with your way of thinking. It seems to me that this sort of thing can only lead to trouble, to a waste of time and money. This— gadget, for instance.''

"The Scuttler? It's not a gadget," began the Professor.

"No? What's it good for, aside from dumping babies in people's laps?''

"I have already explained—''

"You've already told me that it was a way of demonstrating control operations. I can see that it's very interesting, what with the radar and all the rest of it. But what's it good for?''

"Good for? I don't understand,'' the Professor said, appearing somewhat taken aback.

"There you are. You don't know,'' snapped Mr. String. "I'm interested in big stuff, Professor. The space program. Atomic research. Important stuff. Practical research which will give us some live-wire public relations and put Midston on the map. If I were to use your Scudder or whatever it's called as our chief attraction in the Science and Industry Fair, we'd be laughed out of the fair grounds. That is, if anyone paid any attention to it at all.''

He went to the door. "I must warn you, Professor,'' he said, "we want men who will pull their weight on our team. I can't waste any more time here. Good day."

He jammed his hat on, and left.

Danny let out his breath in a long sigh. He stole a glance at Professor Bullfinch. He had never seen the scientist look so stern, and at the same time so sad.

"Never mind, Professor," he said, in a small voice. "It doesn't matter . . . does it?"

Professor Bullfinch started. He put an arm around Danny's shoulders, and gave the boy a hug.

"You remember the fable about the frog who tried to puff himself up to the size of an ox?" he said. "No, it doesn't matter a bit— except to the frog. Come on, let's see whether Emmet has recovered from his awful experience."

"I don't think riding on the Scuttler was so awful," Danny said. "I wouldn't mind doing it myself."

"I didn't mean that," chuckled Professor Bullfinch. "I meant tasting Mr. String."

6
That Glazed Look

Mr. String's visit left an air of depression over the Bullfinch household, in spite of the Professor's attempts to shrug it off. But fortunately for Danny, he was too busy during the next two days to think much about the matter, for Joe's play had its dress rehearsal, and then on the following evening its performance.

Naturally, at the dress rehearsal, everything went wrong. John Karrell, who usually knew his lines perfectly, forgot every speech he had to utter; Ricky Benjamin, who took the part of the robot, X-5, slipped while climbing in through the window and fell flat on the rocket ship's control board, mashing it completely out of shape. The curtain got stuck, and at one point there was a short circuit and every light blew out. Joe tore his hair and groaned and threatened to lock himself in a closet until all was over.

But somehow things sorted themselves out. Danny and Johnny Atwood quickly repaired the control panel. Teddy Ruml, the stage manager, fixed the curtain and got the lights working again. The actors promised to behave themselves, and Mrs. Pearson arrived just as the rehearsal was ending bearing a huge chocolate cake and several thermos containers of strawberry punch with which to cheer up the cast and stage crew.

Then, as is usually the case, the performance itself went off without a flaw. The auditorium was filled with school children and their families, and all the smaller ones screamed in the most gratifying way at each appearance of the shining robot. Dr. Ziv was roundly booed, and the heroes were greeted with cheers. And when, at the beginning of the second act, the curtain opened to reveal the rocky landscape of the moon bathed in silver light against a black sky—an effect Johnny Atwood had planned and carried out carefully—there was enormous applause. At the end of the show, Miss Arnold, their teacher, hugged Joe and told him how talented he was, and many of the parents came up to congratulate him.

"Just the same," Joe remarked to Danny, "I don't think I'll ever go through this again. I'm too young to have gray hair."

But his face was split by an enormous smile of pleasure as he said it.

Things could now return to normal. On Saturday, the stage crew dismantled the sets, returned the various properties they had borrowed for the show, and cleaned up the auditorium.

"Now," Joe said, as they took a last look around the stage to be sure that everything was tidy, "the slide downhill begins, towards exams and the summer vacation."

"Yes," said Danny, "and now I've got time to worry a little."

"Worry about what?"

"Professor Bullfinch, of course. He tries not to show it, but I know he's very upset."

"You mean after that day with Mr. String?"

"Uh-huh. I heard him talking about it with Dr. Miller. He said that maybe Dr. Miller was right, and that Mr. String might be able to change the tone of the whole university, in spite of the president, Dr. Richards, and the other trustees. And worst of all, he said that maybe it was time for him to retire altogether from teaching. . . ." Danny sighed. "The trouble is that I keep thinking it was all my fault, Joe."

"How could it be your fault? You didn't put Emmet on top of the Scuttler; Irene did. And it's not even her fault. She didn't know the Professor was going to whistle for the thing."

"But if I hadn't sprinkled that pepper around, nothing would have happened in the first place. I'm always falling into these things. I don't *mean* to. When will I ever learn to think first and do something afterward?"

"A good question," said Joe. "And it deserves a good answer. Never. Next question."

"Oh, you can kid around," Danny said, moodily. "It doesn't concern you."

"Hey, none of that!" Joe took his friend's arm. "Why not? We're buddies, aren't we? Sure it concerns me."

"I'm sorry, Joe." Danny was instantly contrite.

"Aw, forget it. It's just that you *are* headstrong, but at the same time I don't think you ought to feel everything's your fault."

"Well, maybe not."

"Sure not. When an accident happens, a lot of people share the blame. Now look, I've got to go home because it's lunchtime. But let's meet this afternoon and go for a hike. Okay?"

"Okay. And thanks, Joe. For a gloomy guy you do manage to cheer me up," grinned Danny.

He went off home feeling considerably lighter of heart. When he opened the front door, he heard music coming from the living room. He peeped inside. Professor Bullfinch was holding a small violin, which appeared very odd to Dan, since the Professor's usual instrument was a huge bull fiddle on which in his spare time he played growlsome pieces. On the floor, cross-legged in front of him, was an audience of one.

Emmet wasn't wearing his submarine sweater today. Instead, he was smartly dressed in gray flannel shorts and a blue jacket. He looked, Danny thought, surprisingly clean and shiny, more ordinary somehow. He was staring up at the Professor and his violin with fascination.

"Hullo, Dan," said the Professor. "Come on in."

"What's happened to your bull fiddle?" Danny dropped into an armchair. "It looks as though you washed it and it shrunk."

"Ah, I couldn't use the bull fiddle for this experiment," said the Professor. "I've been playing duets with young Emmet, and the bull fiddle's tones are too deep for him."

"Duets with Emmet? I didn't know he could play an instrument."

"Neither did he," chuckled the Professor. "Just listen."

He drew the bow across one of the strings, producing a high, slightly sour note. Then he paused. "Go on, my boy," he said. "Sing."

Emmet opened his mouth. A soulful look came into his eyes. He uttered a high, piercing shriek that almost split Danny's eardrums. From the violin came the same note the Professor had just played, only more faintly, as if a ghost had drawn an invisible bow across the strings.

Danny rubbed his forehead. "Golly," he said. "How does he do it?"

"Sympathetic vibration," replied the Professor. "This boy has remarkable vocal cords. He can make a sound intense enough to move the fiddle string. And when he gets just the right frequency it makes the string vibrate at the note I play."

Danny frowned. "I know what frequency is in electricity," he said. "But I'm not sure I know what you mean when you say frequency in talking about sound."

"Well, as you know," said the Professor, "sound is a disturbance of molecules. Imagine a curtain made out of long strings of beads. When you utter a sound, you push the string nearest you. The beads swing and touch the next strand, which swings back and forth, touching the next and making it move. So a kind of wave of movement passes along the whole curtain. What we call *pitch* is the number of times this wave of motion goes past any given point in one second."

"How frequently it goes past?" Danny said.

"Exactly. That's why it's called frequency. The *speed* of sound, normally, in air, is always the same—"

"Eleven hundred feet per second," Danny put in.

"Just so. But the more of those waves there are going past a point in one second, the higher the frequency. Now Emmet can send thousands of cycles, or waves of movement along the bead curtain, every second. We can hear up to perhaps 20,000 cycles per second. But he can screech in a pitch around 30,000 or 40,000, where dogs can hear him, but we can't."

"Gee, he's got hidden talents all right,"

Danny said, looking admiringly at Emmet. "And now you're trying to teach him to play the violin with no hands? What a concert he could give!"

They were both laughing at the image when Irene came in.

"I'll have to take Emmet now, Professor," she said. "Uncle George says it's time for them to start for New York, and Aunt Joan wants to wash his face and brush his hair."

"Omeepa," Emmet protested.

"Yes, you do need to," said Irene, taking his hand. "You're like that little boy in the *Peanuts* cartoon who gets dirty just sitting still."

She looked at Danny and the Professor. "You're both looking merry," she said. "Has Mr. String changed his mind?"

The Professor's face fell, and he sighed. "I'm afraid not," he replied. "It's really not his fault, you understand. He's acting from the best motives. He wants to do what he thinks is right for Midston. It would make it easier for everyone if I could find an idea that would satisfy him!"

He shook himself. "Well, never mind. Good-bye, Emmet. I hope you have a good journey home. It was pleasant to know you."

Gravely, he shook hands with the child. "I must come to New York some day and play some more duets with you." Then he chuckled. "I'll certainly never forget that terribly funny moment when Emmet came sailing in on the Scuttler," he said. "He was delivered to us like—like a ham sandwich in an Automat cafeteria."

"None of us will ever forget it," Irene laughed. "Come on, Emmet. Say good-bye to Danny."

Emmet stood obediently before Dan with his hand held out. But Danny was staring into space with a peculiar blank look in his eyes and his mouth hanging open like a bureau drawer which has been pulled out too far.

"Danny," Irene said. She squinted at him. "Danny, wake up! What's the matter with you?"

Professor Bullfinch inspected the boy, and nodded. "I know that glazed look," he said. "It means that some sort of wild but entertaining notion is revolving in his head. Come, now, Danny. Out with it."

Danny blinked. He clapped his hands over his mouth. Then, through giggles of joy, he blurted, "Listen! This is a wonderful idea. I'll bet Mr. String will love it."

"Speak," said the Professor. "What is it?"

"What you just said—delivered him like a sandwich," Danny chortled. "That's it."

"I must be getting old and rusty," said the Professor, frowning. "I fail to get it. Do you mean that we should deliver Mr. String a sandwich? Make Emmet into a sandwich? What?"

"I mean that if the Scuttler could deliver Emmet, it ought to be able to deliver anything. Sandwiches—cake—tea—dinner. A robot butler, that's what I mean," cried Danny. "A *Scuttler*-butler!"

7
Mr. String
Is Pleased

"Well," said Mr. String, "it had better be good."

Professor Bullfinch had wasted no time. He had telephoned Mr. String at once, telling him that he wanted to show him a particularly interesting use for the Scuttler. Pointing out that he was a busy man and had five other meetings to attend, Mr. String said that he could squeeze in a quick visit then and there, and would be at the Bullfinch house in ten minutes.

"That gives us just enough time," said the Professor. "We'll serve him coffee and cake."

Mrs. Dunn was out doing her shopping, but there was some coffee left from breakfast in the electric percolator, and it took only a minute or two to get it hot. Irene bore Emmet off, bemoaning the fact that she couldn't stay and commanding Danny to give her a full report of what happened. The Professor brought the Scuttler into the kitchen and he and Dan put a large silver tray on top of it. They set the tray with the best coffee cups, sugar and cream, a plateful of cookies, and a thermos jug full of hot coffee. They wedged the kitchen door open and went into the living room.

They had finished just in time. Mr. String's long, low car drove up to the curb, he fought his way out of it with many puffs and groans, and came swiftly up the front steps with his briefcase flapping. Danny let him in.

"You again, eh? The rest of the kids here too?" said Mr. String.

"No, sir. Nobody's here but Professor Bullfinch," said Danny, politely. "I won't be in your way, sir. I hope you won't mind if I just stand quietly in a corner and watch."

Mr. String shook hands with Professor Bullfinch, who came from the living room where he had been putting away his bull fiddle. "No nonsense this time, I hope."

"Just come in and sit down, Mr. String," said the Professor. "I think I have what you're looking for. Would you like a cup of coffee?''

''I rarely drink the stuff,'' said Mr. String.

Danny and the Professor exchanged horrified glances.

Mr. String looked at his wrist watch. ''But if it's ready,'' he said, ''I'll have a cup.''

''Phew!'' The Professor smiled. ''It is ready. I'll tell the butler to bring it in.'' He picked up the Scuttler's control box.

''Butler? I didn't know you had a butler,'' said Mr. String, suspiciously.

''I do now,'' said the Professor, his eyes twinkling. ''Alfred, bring the coffee. Now. *Go!*''

They waited expectantly. Suddenly from the kitchen came a shrill scream. Then a thumping crash, which shook the very floor.

''What on earth—?'' the Professor began.

''Mom!'' cried Danny, his face white.

Together, they sprinted out of the room. Mr. String gaped after them, and then decided to follow.

The kitchen door was closed. Professor Bullfinch yanked it open.

The Scuttler came sailing triumphantly out. It dodged between the Professor and Danny, side-stepped Mr. String, and bearing aloft its load of coffee and cookies, vanished into the living room in search of the control box which was still sending out a signal from the end table where the Professor had dropped it.

Danny was already in the kitchen. His mother stood looking ruefully down at a large shopping bag which lay split at her feet spilling canned goods, broken eggs, bread, and jars of jelly all over the floor.

"Are you all right, Mom?" Danny said.

"Oh, yes," said Mrs. Dunn, bitterly. "Only frightened out of my wits and with the floor ankle-deep in groceries. Euclid Bullfinch," she went on, turning on the Professor with her most severe expression, "what kind of prank was that to play on an unsuspecting woman? I never expected to see my best silver coffee tray go traveling under its own steam that way!"

"I'm terribly sorry, Mrs. Dunn," said the Professor. "I didn't expect you home until later. And the kitchen door should have been open. I can't understand—"

"Why, when I came in I heard you talking in the living room, and I had seen the car out front," Mrs. Dunn said, "so I closed the door so as not to disturb you. Then I had just picked up my bag of groceries and was about to put it on the counter next to the refrigerator when the coffee tray went waltzing off."

"Incredible!" said Mr. String. They had forgotten him.

His large red face glowed like an angry planet. He shook his head. "Never in all my experience," he growled. "Never . . . have . . . I . . . seen . . . anything . . . like . . . this!" A shake of the head went with each word. "Children falling into laps. Sulphuric acid. Coffee trays. Shopping bags. Confusion. Absolute, *utter,* CONFUSION!"

"Come, come, Mr. String," said the Professor, gently. "You're making too much of this. It was a slight accident. But you saw the Scuttler in action. It's now in the living room

ready to serve you your coffee. If we had only had an automatic door which could have opened for it, all would have been well. Except for poor Mrs. Dunn's astonishment, of course.''

"I don't see. . . ." Mr. String was beginning.

He was interrupted by a shout from Danny.

"I've got it! Don't say anything! I've got it!''

Mr. String shrank back, quivering. "Good heavens," he said, "what has he got? A fit! He's got a fit! Get a doctor. Keep him away from me, whatever it is."

Danny was capering around as if, in fact, he did have some sort of rare disease that kept him dancing.

"Danny!" Mrs. Dunn exclaimed. "Stop it this instant."

Then, at last, he calmed down. "But listen," he begged, "I'm not crazy. Only I just had this marvelous, perfectly great idea. Mr. String, it's just what you want—just the thing for an exhibition for Midston's part in the Science Fair."

"Is he foaming at the mouth?" mumbled Mr. String, cowering behind his briefcase.

"Not yet," said the Professor, dryly. "Go on, Dan."

"Why, you said that if we had had an automatic door to open for the Scuttler, there'd have been no problem. And I thought, well, why not an automatic kitchen, too, to prepare the coffee and cookies and put them on the Scuttler? And why not an automatic dishwasher to wash up afterwards. All these things are in existence now, they don't have to be invented. But—why not an *automatic house?*"

"Now, Dan, don't let your imagination run away with you, dear," said Mrs. Dunn. "I don't think Mr. String really cares about—"

"Just a moment, Madam." Mr. String had lost his frightened look, had straightened up, and was once again tall, stout, pompous, and businesslike. "Let the boy continue. I have always believed in encouraging young people who are—hrrmph!—interested in science. Well, young man?"

"Why, in an automatic house you could show off all the newest developments in electronic control systems. Not just the Scuttler, but all sorts of things. Things already in existence, like an oven which prepares food and cooks it at the right heat for the right length of time. Sure, but also new things, things that would have to be developed, like—like—oh, an automatic bathtub for instance."

"An automatic bathtub?" Mr. String blinked.

"Uh-huh. Say it's Saturday night, time for a bath. At the right time, the bathtub fills with water, the soap flips into it, a washcloth comes down into position, and a voice calls you and says, 'Your bath is ready.' "

"My word!" said Mr. String. "Not bad. Did you just think of that?"

"Yes, sir. I'll bet the scientists at Midston would think of lots more ideas. And you could have the different departments get together and contribute, and so it would be a real project for the whole University."

"Excellent," said Mr. String. He whirled around, waving a finger in Professor Bullfinch's face. "You see, Professor? I've always said that it pays to encourage youngsters in science. After all, they are the men and women of the future, aren't they? This is a magnificent idea. I can see it now, the center of the fair— the object of everyone's attention—the *Midston University Automatic House!*"

He grabbed the Professor's hand and pumped it. "I must be going," he said. "There are a thousand things to do to organize this. I must discuss it with the other trustees and with Dr. Richards. I'm sure they'll all see the importance of this project. I intend to push this thing through. It's exactly what I've been looking for."

The Professor took him to the door. There, Mr. String paused. "You see, Professor," he said, in a kindly tone, "it's a matter of keeping one's eyes and ears open. You scientists get so wrapped up in your work that you don't pay attention to new things. But I always keep an open mind, it's the secret of my success. And I knew that if I thought about it long enough, the right idea would come to me."

"It will be a lesson to me," said the Professor, keeping a perfectly straight face.

"Good. Good. Er—there's one thing more. I expect Dr. Richards will want to call a faculty meeting about this matter. We can hardly invite a child to it. But perhaps now that I've broken the ground for you, you can talk to the boy and—ah—see if he has any more good ideas. An automatic bathtub. Heavens!"

"I'll try, Mr. String," the Professor said, seriously. "But as you have seen for yourself, Danny is a very quiet boy. He doesn't talk much, and he's shy and retiring."

Mr. String looked sharply at the Professor's innocent face. "Hm! Yes," he said. "Well,

I've done the basic work, Professor. I leave the rest to you."

The Professor closed the door after him, and fell back against it, helpless with laughter.

"He liked it," Danny said, grinning.

"Yes, my boy. He did indeed. You were right."

"I don't think I understood everything that was going on," said Mrs. Dunn, in a bewildered voice.

"I'll explain in a moment, my dear Mrs. Dunn," said the Professor. "But first, I think the Scuttler is still waiting patiently for us, and the coffee in the thermos is undoubtedly still hot enough to drink. Shall we go?"

He offered one arm to Danny and the other to Mrs. Dunn, and bore them off with him to the living room.

8
"A Machine for Living"

The next few months were busy ones for Professor Bullfinch, and there were some exciting moments for Danny as the project began to take shape.

As Mr. String had hoped, the large open meadow near the University had been chosen as the site for the fair. Very soon surveyors were at work with their telescopes and plumb lines, marking out the streets and the exhibition areas. There was to be a huge main tent full of booths in which equipment of all sorts would be shown. A great number of smaller tents, trailers, or temporary buildings would house

displays from schools and colleges. Several
large companies which seemed to have letters
instead of names—IBM, GM, ICE—began the
construction of special buildings in which to
demonstrate their work: there would be computers, astronomical apparatus, chemical and
biological exhibits, material from every field
of science. A large space was given over to
Midston University, to be used for the Automatic House. The date of the fair was announced: it would open on July 21 and run for
two weeks, and it would be attended by all
sorts of important people from every part of
the country.

Danny was invited to one of the first faculty
meetings at which plans for the Automatic
House were discussed.

"I hope you realize," said Professor Bullfinch, as they walked across the campus together, "that this is an almost unheard-of
thing, Dan. But when it became known that
the idea was yours, the faculty members felt
that the least they could do was to let you come
to the meeting. I hope, my dear boy, that you
will manage not to jump up and yell out any
ideas that come to you. Not that I want to stop
your imagination working, but some of our
professors are rather old and easily shocked."

"I'll be good," Danny promised. "But if I do get an idea . . ."

"Write it down on a piece of paper," said the Professor hastily. "That's always the best procedure."

The faculty meeting was held in a large, dark-paneled conference room whose tall windows looked out to the magnificent view of Sugarloaf Mountain. Many of the heads of departments came over to shake hands with Danny; many, who were friends of Professor Bullfinch's, already knew him and joked with him. Dr. Richards, the president of the University, warned him with a kindly chuckle that if he didn't watch out he might grow up to be a college president some day. Even Mr. String, who was present as the sponsor of the project, smiled a rather tight smile and nodded to him. Professor Bullfinch took a seat near the back of the room and Danny made himself comfortable in one of the brown leather chairs beside him. The room quickly filled, and soon curls of tobacco smoke mingled with the invigorating odors of polished wood and old leather.

Dr. Richards opened the meeting. After talking about the fair and its general arrangements, he introduced Mr. String, who got up, cleared his throat, and said, "You've all had a chance to think about our project, the Midston Automatic House. It is going to be the Biggest Attraction of the fair." As he spoke, everyone could hear the capital letters forming. "I look to it to put Midston University over with a Bang, to give us the sort of Live-wire Publicity a university needs if it is to find Support and Money for all its programs."

The head of the English department, a thin, elegant man with silvery hair, raised his hand. "As I understand it," he said, "this house is a kind of display of gadgets. It may be an entertaining project for the physicists and engineers, but I don't see the point of the rest of us being here. Why English professors, or art instructors? What have we got to do with it?"

Mr. String said, "I think I'll let Professor Bullfinch answer that, since his—er—hrrmph!—it was more or less his idea."

Professor Bullfinch took his pipe out of his mouth. "It wasn't," he replied. "I think most of you know whose idea it was. However, I don't mind answering. The house is *not* going to be a display of gadgets. It is going to be a house. It will be an example of how modern technology can make living easier. I admit it will also be a showcase for certain interesting ideas on the uses of automatic control systems. But it's as a house that we should think of it— a place for people to live in. It will need books, pictures on the walls, music. Seems to me your department and the others must have some notions about this sort of thing."

"It's true, I do have some ideas," put in the head of the art department. "I've often thought that it might be pleasant to have a file of color transparencies of great paintings in one's house, and a framed screen on one wall. Then, every day or every week, as the mood took you, you'd project a different picture on the screen. A home art gallery!"

"Not bad," said the head of the English department. "I've often wondered why no one makes films of Shakespeare plays available for home movie projectors. Imagine a complete library of Shakespeare on records, and film, as well as in books!"

"And reference books," cried the head of the French department. "Think of them. You know what a trouble it is to look something up in the huge large encyclopedia? Ah, but we could have microfilm encyclopedias, and some sort of a system like these computer gentlemen have, so that when you wanted to look something up—pif!—you put it in a viewer and find what you want at once."

"Well, there you are, gentlemen," said Mr. String. "You see, there are all sorts of ideas which will occur to you. We want you to get busy. Within the next couple of weeks send all those notions—no matter how crazy they seem to you—to the faculty committee, which will work closely with me. That committee is headed by Professor Bullfinch and Dr. Miller."

"One more point," said the head of the mathematics department, patting her hair back into place. "Surely you don't expect us to design and furnish this house?"

"No indeed," said Mr. String. He slapped his briefcase, which lay on the table before him. "I have already arranged with several local merchants and manufacturers to loan us furnishings or make special equipment for us. As for the design of the house itself, we plan to hire a professional architect.''

Danny almost jumped up. Fortunately, he remembered what Professor Bullfinch had told him, and kept his seat. He fumbled through his pockets for a piece of paper, and at last succeeded in finding an old shopping list his mother had given him. Quickly, he wrote something on the back of it. He tugged Professor Bullfinch's sleeve and passed him the piece of paper.

''Read it out loud,'' he whispered.

Professor Bullfinch said, ''Excuse me, Mr. String, but I have a communication here which I'd like to read.''

''Go ahead,'' said Mr. String.

''One head of lettuce,'' read the Professor, ''a loaf of white bread, a dozen eggs. Dear me, no, that's not it. Excuse me.'' He turned the paper over. ''Uncle George,'' he read.

''I beg your pardon?'' said Mr. String. Titters went through the room.

''George Miller, of course!'' the Professor said. ''A fine thought. As I have been reminded by Danny, Dr. Miller's brother is an architect and a very good one. Furthermore, he knows something about our researches. He'd be the ideal man to do the job if we can persuade him to take it."

"I'm sure he'll be delighted," said Dr. Miller. "He's always looking for excuses to get out of the city. We can put him up at our house when the time comes."

"Good," said Mr. String. "As one of the committee heads, Dr. Miller, suppose you write to him. Well, ladies and gentlemen, that's it. Put your thinking caps on, and let's all Get Behind this Project and Push."

"But not too hard a push or we might fall on our faces," murmured the head of the English department to Professor Bullfinch.

As they walked home, the Professor said, "That was good thinking, Dan. I can't imagine why George Miller's name hadn't occurred to me. I'll be glad to see him and his wife again, and of course little Emmet. Pehaps I'll have the chance to do a bit more research into the peculiarities of that child's vocal cords."

"Yes, and I'll bet Joe will be tickled to see his taster again," Danny giggled.

At lunch, they told Mrs. Dunn about the meeting. She laughed with them over the Professor's reading her shopping list, and was pleased that Irene's Uncle George might be designing the Automatic House.

"That house sounds just a wee bit scarey, though," she said, as she gathered up the plates.

"Scarey? Why, Mom?" asked Danny.

"I seem to remember someone saying, 'A house is a machine for living.' That's what this reminds me of." Mrs. Dunn shook her head vigorously. "My house isn't a machine and I don't want it to be."

"That isn't what the phrase means," objected the Professor. "The famous architect Le Corbusier used it, and he meant that a house ought to be built for the greatest convenience and ease of the people who live in it. We build machines to do a job properly, so why not houses? For instance, a house with a big picture window that just looks out at another house instead of a view, isn't functioning properly."

Mrs. Dunn put the dishes in the sink. "There's no arguing with that," she said. "It's quite true. But I think you can get carried away by the idea that having lots of gadgets in a house will turn it into a home. The thing that turns even a hole in the ground into a home is having people live in it and drop their clothes and belongings around and put their souvenirs about the place."

"I think we agree with each other, Mrs.

Dunn," said the Professor, leaning back in his chair. "Perhaps the thing that puts you off is our calling it an *automatic* house. But that was Mr. String's phrase, and he's enchanted with it."

"But gee, Mom," Danny said, "you wouldn't want to throw out all the new inventions would you? From what you said, it sounds as though you'd want to get rid of washing machines and freezers and all the rest."

"No indeed. Those things are all useful tools. But I want them to be just that—tools I use, and nothing else. Things I run for my convenience, not things that run *me*."

Mrs. Dunn rested her hands on her hips and gazed around her cozy kitchen. "Once you start trying to save work by putting in machines, you may find you're spending all your time taking care of the machines and not getting any fun out of your work," she said. "This kitchen is my studio—my laboratory, just like your laboratory, Professor. Would you want an automatic laboratory?"

"Heavens, what an idea!" Professor Bullfinch laughed. "Next you'll be suggesting an automatic professor. I see your point, Mrs. Dunn. But remember, the Midston Automatic

House *isn't* a home, really. It's a demonstration. We'll never know how it would serve as a home since no one will ever live in it.''

"Too bad," mumbled Danny, under his breath. "But why not? Why shouldn't someone try living in it?''

"What did you say, dear?" asked his mother.

"Oh—nothing, Mom," said Danny.

9
Leaving It
to Luck

The weeks flew by. The fair sprang up as if by
magic: first some pegs and posts, then some
scaffolding and tent poles, and then, overnight
it seemed, tents, signs, fences, and brightly
painted buildings. For Danny and his friends
school went at a slower pace. But suddenly it
was examination time, and then they had put
away their books and found summer stretching
ahead of them, leading to the day when the fair
would open.

On the evening of July 18, Professor Bullfinch came home in high good humor.

"Everything's ready," he said, rubbing his
hands. "And everything works."

"You've been at the Hardware Shop?" Danny said. It was their pet name for the Automatic House.

"Yes. With Mr. String, the other members of the committee, and the three directors of the fair. A private showing, as it were. We tested everything in the place. Works like a charm. It may very well turn out that Mr. String's somewhat extravagant prediction may be true: this may be the biggest attraction after all."

He took out his wallet. "I have something for you, Dan."

"For me? What is it?"

The Professor handed him three pieces of cardboard. "Special exhibitor's passes. One for you, one for Irene, and one for Joe."

"I don't understand. What's an exhibitor's pass? I'm not exhibiting anything."

"These passes let you go into the fair any time you want to, free of charge. They are a present from the directors."

"The directors? Of the fair?" Danny stared.

"Absolutely. One of them is an old friend of mine, Dr. Sundergard. When I told him the whole story about the house, he insisted that you three should be suitably rewarded."

"Why, Danny! That's a great honor," said

Mrs. Dunn. "You must write to Dr. Sundergard and thank him."

"It won't be necessary, Mrs. Dunn," said the Professor. "Danny will see the directors on the opening day, and he can thank them then. We're all going to the opening ceremony—you and the Millers and the Pearsons."

"Oh, boy!" Danny cried. "Do the others know yet?"

"Not yet. I thought I'd leave that to you. You can phone them."

"Why don't I run over and give them their tickets?"

"It's a little late for that, Dan," said Mrs. Dunn. "Do it tomorrow morning."

"Aw, gee, Mom!" Danny protested, but Mrs. Dunn had her way.

Early next morning, however, Danny met with the other two and solemnly handed them their passes.

"Can we look at anything we like, or do we just have to go to the Midston House?" asked Joe, examining his pass.

"We can go anywhere and do anything. It sort of makes us officials," Danny said proudly. He looked at his bit of pasteboard. "I wonder . . ." he added.

"What do you wonder, O Wondrous One?" said Joe. "Whether we can sell these to somebody and make enough money to take a rocket to the moon?"

"No, I was wondering whether we can get into the fair *before* it opens," Danny replied.

"What for?" asked Irene.

"Well," Danny began, slowly, "once, when this whole thing started, my mother and Professor Bullfinch were having an argument about houses and machines. And the Professor said they'd never be able to settle it—about the Automatic House—because nobody'd ever live in it. And I've been thinking. . . ."

"Don't tell me!" Joe exclaimed, clutching his head. "I'm not, repeat NOT, going to go live in that house with you. In the first place, with people walking through it we'd never have any privacy."

"Take it easy, Joe," Danny laughed. "I've just been thinking that it would be nice to get into the place and see it, and try it out, *before* all the people start marching through. See, once the crowds begin coming in, it's just an exhibit. But right now, it's a house, an empty house sort of waiting for visitors. It would be fun to try out whether it could be lived in like a real home."

Irene pinched her lower lip, thoughtfully. "Do you think it would be right to go in, now, Danny?"

"Why not? It's as much mine as anybody's. And we wouldn't do any harm. Just walk around and look, and maybe see how the things work."

He thrust his hands deep into his pockets. "Tell you what," he said. "Let's leave it to luck. Let's take some sandwiches and walk over to the fair. If we can get in with these passes, we'll just go *look* at the house. And if we can get into it—why, that'll show we're *meant* to go in. Then we can have our lunch there and spend a couple of hours. And if we can't get in, well then, we've had a walk. Okay?"

Irene squinched up her nose and peered at him through half-closed eyes. "You know what?" she said. "You're a very persuasive boy. You'll probably grow up to be a politician or a salesman, instead of a physicist." She shrugged. "All right. It's a lovely day and I feel like a stroll."

Joe sighed. "I suppose I'll have to come along, to make sure you two don't get into trouble," he said.

"Fine," said Danny. "Let's all go home and

make sandwiches, and we'll meet at the corner of Washington Avenue in fifteen minutes.''

Their passes got them into the fair without trouble. The guard at the main gate looked at the cards and grinned. ''Goin' to check your atomic pile, kids?'' he said.

''As a matter of fact, we are going to check system response to acoustical input at various frequencies,'' said Danny, coolly.

The guard stared after them as they walked past him. ''Well, what about that?'' he asked, of nobody in particular. ''Kids nowadays!''

''What did that mean what you said, Dan?'' Joe asked, after a moment.

Danny winked. ''Nothing much—that we're going to talk to the machines in different ways and see what they say back to us. I just wanted to give him something to think about.''

The fair grounds were nearly empty. Here and there, last-minute touches were being given to some of the exhibits, and through the glass walls of the IBM building a group of men could be seen gathered around the console of a giant computer. Near the center of the fair a large sign announced MIDSTON UNIVER-SITY AUTOMATIC HOUSE—THE HOUSE OF TOMORROW, and in smaller letters, *Demonstration of Automatic Control Systems prepared by the Faculty of the University: Architect—George Miller.* A high wooden fence surrounded the whole thing, and above it foliage and the V-shaped roof of the house itself could just be glimpsed.

"Looks impressive, doesn't it?" said Irene.

"Looks locked," said Joe.

There was a large padlock on the gate next to the ticket window.

"Well, I guess that does it," Irene said, rather sadly. "I suppose we weren't meant to go in after all."

"Let's just walk around the fence," said Danny. "You never know."

They followed the fence. Halfway round, they came to a small door. It was marked STAFF ONLY. Danny tried the latch. It clicked, and the door swung open.

"Aha!" he crowed. "People are always putting big locks on the fronts of things and then forgetting about the little back doors."

The house was set in the midst of a garden, or rather several gardens. There was a rock garden, a rose garden, a garden of old-fashioned flowers, and an herb garden. Small groves of birches or bright crimson Japanese maples separated them, and flagstone paths led from one to another.

The house itself was simple but striking. Gray shingles and solid, stained wood alternated with walls of solid glass, which looked out at the different gardens. A roof like a pair of wings gave it a strange lightness and grace.

The three went to the front door. Joe reached for the door knob, pawed the air, and blinked. There was no door knob.

Danny snickered. He touched a button set in a small box next to the door. A deep, metallic voice said, "O-pen." The door slid to one side.

Joe twitched uneasily. "Spooky," he said. "It reminds me of a movie I once saw called *I Was Dracula's Date*."

"It's very simple," said Danny. "The door of the house is keyed to that word and to a certain pitch of the voice. Since there'll be lots of people with different voices coming here, they thought it would be best to have a *voder*—

a mechanical voice, just for the demonstration, so everyone can see how the door works. Come on, let's go in.''

''Does it close the same way?'' Irene asked.

''Yes.'' He scratched his head thoughtfully. ''I suppose everyone who lives in a house like this will have to carry a portable *voder* instead of keys.''

There were only four rooms: an L-shaped living room, a large kitchen-dining room, a bedroom, and a bathroom. All the colors were soft and rich, the expanse of glass gave the

rooms great airiness, and the whole look of the place was comfortable and inviting.

"When the fair opens, there'll be guides here," Danny told the others. "They'll be college students who will be stationed all over the house, and who will explain how everything works. And then, you can see that there are some notices which describe servomechanisms and tell how some of the things operate."

"It just looks like an ordinary house to me," Joe said. "A little on the fancy side, maybe—"

"You don't know how fancy," Danny chuckled. "Let me show you something."

He went to a round knob set into a wall. "Now," he said, "you're looking out of the living room window at that patch of garden and trees. You get tired of the view and you decide to change it. What do you do?"

"You go outside," Joe said, promptly, "and dig up everything and move it around."

"Nope. You move the house around," said Danny.

He twisted the knob. At once, with a faint hum, the floor moved slightly under their feet. Staring through the large pane that was one whole wall of the room, they saw that the house was turning. The birches outside seemed to flow slowly past, and now instead of the rose garden, they were looking at a hump-backed chunk of limestone at the beginning of the rock garden.

Danny touched the knob. "How do you like that?" he asked, as the house came to a halt. "A change of scene any time you want it."

"Suppose somebody comes to visit?" said Irene.

"Oh, the walk runs from the front gate all around the house. No matter where the front door is, a visitor can always find it," said Dan.

"That's nice," Joe remarked. "Because I think we have a visitor now."

A small figure had appeared on the top of the limestone rock. Like Hillary at the summit of Mt. Everest, Emmet stood victoriously looking about him, his round face more puddinglike than ever, his round blue eyes calmly curious. He saw them through the window, wiped his nose on his sleeve, and waved. It was too warm for his submarine sweater, but he was wearing an old Navy denim shirt of his father's which came down to his ankles.

Irene ran to the door. "Emmet! Come here this minute," she called.

When he appeared at the door, she grabbed him. "Oh, you awful child," she said. "Did you follow us?"

He nodded solemnly.

"And of course you didn't tell anybody. No, how could you? Aunt Joan will be hopping mad. And at me, I'll bet."

"Omma gape O," said Emmet, cheerfully.

"You want to play with Joe," Irene translated. "That's fine. Heads will roll—! What'll I do, Danny. Shall I take him home?"

"Ope," said Emmet.

"I'll bet that means 'No,' " said Joe, with a grin. "Wicked brat! Frankenstein's baby had nothing on you."

He patted Emmet absentmindedly on the head.

"I know. I'll call home," Irene said. "Where's the phone?"

"That thing." Danny pointed to a smoothly polished wooden cabinet with a metal disk up-ended on the top of it. There was a glass plate in the front of the cabinet. There were also two buttons, one marked *On*, the other *Off*.

"I suppose I push the *On* button," said Irene, doing so.

"Hello," said the telephone. In the glass plate appeared a picture of a smiling woman.

"Hello," Irene said, without thinking.

"This is a dummy telephone, for demonstration purposes,'' said the woman. ''You are watching and listening to a tape recording. The telephone of the future will have an optional live image of the person you are talking to—''

''A dummy!'' Irene pushed the *Off* switch crossly. ''It's very interesting, but what *am* I to do about Emmet?''

Joe fished out a stick of chewing gum and gave it to Emmet, who was standing as close to him as he could get. ''I suppose we'd better take him home after all,'' he said. ''Let's just look around a bit more.''

Emmet had peeled the wrapper from his gum. He tossed the paper on the floor. There was a *snap!* An opening appeared in the baseboard of one wall, and out of it rushed a shining little metal monster. It was about a foot square. Two silvery rods rose out of the top like the antennae of an insect. It shot over to the gum wrapper. One end of it opened, there was a gulping noise, and the paper disappeared. The machine whizzed backward into its cave, and the panel snapped behind it.

But before it had vanished, disaster struck. As the mobile vacuum cleaner came towards him, Emmet gave a squeak of dismay and tried to climb for safety up the nearest tall object.

Together they toppled backward

That happened to be Joe. He staggered under the weight of the clawing child, and together they toppled backward. They crashed into the wall, next to the still open front door.

The whole room shook under the impact. And the door slid shut with a sharp, ominous *click*.

10
Emmet Speaks

Danny and Irene ran to help. They pulled Joe to his feet and untangled him from Emmet. Emmet was sniveling slightly but unhurt. Joe had nothing more serious than a bump on the head. They all turned then to look at the closed door.

"I suppose," Irene said, rather uneasily, "there's no problem about opening it? There isn't any door knob on the inside, either."

Danny nodded. "There's a *voder* on this side," he said, with relief, for he hadn't really been sure. He went up to the box, and pressed the button.

"O-pen," said the mechanical voice.

The door didn't stir.

Danny bit his lip. "Something must have been knocked out of whack," he said. Once again, he tried the *voder,* but to no effect.

"Look, I hate to show off my superior intelligence," said Joe, "but didn't someone say something not long ago about people forgetting the little back doors?"

"Of course," said Danny, snapping his fingers. He dashed into the kitchen. There was a back door, by which visitors would leave the house after they had inspected all its wonders. However, unlike the front door, it had an ordinary knob and lock, and had not been forgotten by the technicians, for it was locked up tight and the key had been taken away.

"Well, if girls wore hairpins, and Irene had one, I could pick the lock, if I knew how," Joe observed.

"Now, don't panic," Danny said. "It's simple. We'll just climb out through a window."

But none of the windows were made to open. The big, transparent panes were firmly fixed in place.

"Ooh, that's right," Danny groaned. "The house is air-conditioned. It has thermostats which keep it at the right temperature summer and winter, and ultraviolet rays which kill the germs, and suction ducts which clear the dust out of the air. So the windows never have to open.''

''*I'll* open one,'' Irene said, with the light of battle in her eyes.

Grimly, she pulled off one of her shoes. She went up to the large window over the sink.

''Wait a minute—'' Danny began.

But she had already hit the window as hard as she could with the heel of her shoe. The shoe bounced back and flew out of her hand.

''Plexiglass,'' Danny said, with a shrug. ''Unbreakable.''

''Hmm. People who live in plexiglass houses can throw as many stones as they want to,'' said Joe. ''Okay. So now what? No phone, no way out, and nobody knows we're here.'' He glanced down at Emmet, and then took the little one's grubby hand. ''Come on, buddy. Let's look around, as long as we're stuck here.''

''You're being very calm,'' Danny said. ''This isn't like you, Joe. I guess that rap on the head did something to you. You don't seem to realize. . . .''

Joe shot him a warning look. ''If you want

to know the truth," he said, "I'm aredscay otay eathday." With his free hand, he motioned to Emmet. "Get it?"

Danny nodded. "I get it. Good for you. All right, let's all sit down and have a conference."

The kitchen was a long room, paneled in light stained wood, with a bright floor of black and white squares of linoleum. One end was the cooking area with a stove, counters, and sink, as well as a number of gleaming, colorful machines which were unfamiliar and puzzling. The other, and larger end of the room, had a couple of easy chairs, a long dining table and two benches, some lamps, pictures, books on shelves, and a built-in desk with a console above it like that of a computer, complete with buttons, switches, and colored light panels. The children made themselves comfortable at the table.

"Now," said Danny, trying not to sound worried for Emmet's sake, "we've got a problem. Something's wrong with the machinery that opens the front door. We can't get through the windows, and we can't get out the back door. The fair doesn't open until the day after tomorrow. The fence around this house will keep anyone from seeing us through the windows. We didn't tell anybody where we were going."

"Maybe the Professor will guess," said Irene.

"It's possible," Danny agreed. "Anyway it's not as if we were stranded on top of a mountain, or in a desert. We're okay for food and water, and the place *is* a house after all. We wanted to try living in it—and here we are. Only . . . I would like to get out without them having to come and find us."

His cheeks reddened as he spoke, so that his freckles were swallowed up. "It's sort of embarrassing this way."

Irene nodded. "I know. It's as if we were helpless little kids. Why don't we explore the place, Dan? Maybe we'll get an idea."

"Just what I was going to suggest."

They went into the living room again, and Danny tried the front door once more, but it still would not move. Joe went into the other part of the room formed by the short leg of the L. There were several easy chairs and he sat down on one. At once, the chair folded itself lovingly around him and tipped back; a footrest swung up under his feet, and a cushioned section fitted itself around the back of his head.

A light went on above him, and a neat little panel with a number of buttons on it moved over in front of him.

Joe's first look of surprise had vanished, and he relaxed. "Hey, this is living!" he said. "What a chair! What are all these switches and buttons, Dan?"

"This is what they call the Entertainment Center," Danny said, coming over to stand beside him. "Look, the first button is marked TV. Push it."

Joe did so. A section of the wall in front of him moved silently aside, revealing a television screen.

"The knob next to that button is the remote control station selector and tuner," Danny went on. "The button next to it tunes out the commercials. That was my idea. The next switch calls the Music Section."

"Calls it?" Joe snapped the switch. From its post in a corner, a low cabinet darted out and rolled to his side. Its lid flipped open. Inside was a tape recorder, and on the front of the machine was a list of musical selections, from Beethoven to the Beatles, each with a tiny button next to it.

"Dreamy," said Joe.

"When you press the button next to the selection you want to hear," Danny said, "a tape cartridge slides into place and the music plays until you touch the button again. Then the tape rewinds and the cartridge drops back into its rack. There are lots of other things in the Entertainment Section, too. There's a reference library on microfilm. Another button calls it out. There's a home movie projector and a slide projector. And there's a library of real books—Professor Bullfinch said there couldn't be a substitute for the pleasure of holding a book and reading it. You push a button next to the title you want in the catalog, and the book automatically pops out on the shelf."

He moved away. "None of this is getting us out of here, though," he said. "Pull yourself up, Joe, and let's try the bedroom."

Irene took Emmet's hand, and Joe got reluctantly out of the chair. They went with Dan into the bedroom, through a door that slid aside for them.

Here, there were no windows at all. But on the wall opposite the bed was a softly lighted color photograph of a woodland scene, framed so that it looked as real as a view from a window.

"You can change the picture any time you

like," Dan explained. "It's a projection. You can make it a night scene—with a moon—by changing the lighting. Or you can make it a whole different scene."

"Yes, but suppose when you get up in the morning you want to know what the weather's like outside?" Irene objected.

"Oh, they've thought of that," said Danny. "Next to the bed, here, there's a weather indicator that shows outside temperature, wind velocity, moisture, and so on."

Irene inspected the bed. "Only sheets, no blankets," she said. "I suppose that's because each room has its own temperature control."

Joe lay down. "Nice, too," he said. "What's this gimmick here?" He lazily stretched out a hand and turned a small dial in the wall next to the bed.

"It's . . ." Danny began.

Stirring march music began to play. The bed tilted up sharply and Joe went flying to the floor. A closet opened, and a rack shot out bearing a jacket, a pair of trousers, and a shirt. "Good morning," said a clear, metallic voice.

". . . an alarm clock," Danny finished.

"Blug," announced Emmet.

Joe picked himself up with a disgusted look,

rubbing his back. "Blug is right," he growled. "This house ought to have a first-aid kit in every room."

Danny examined the room. "Nothing in here that gives me any ideas," he said. "What about you others?"

Irene shook her head.

"Maybe we can get that crazy bed to shoot us right through the wall," Joe suggested.

Danny had pushed the rack back into its place in the closet and shut off the alarm. He returned to the living room, and the others trailed after him. He examined the windows there, and then, with the screwdriver blade of his knife unscrewed the cover of the *voder* box beside the door. He peeped into the works and grunted.

"It's beyond me," he said. "I thought maybe there'd be a catch or something that I could release."

"Well, since there's nothing else we can do right now," Irene said, "I suggest we adjourn to that nice dining room part of the kitchen and have lunch. What time is it, I wonder?"

"The time," said a grill on the wall beside her, "is now twelve-fifteen and one quarter."

Irene jumped. "I wish everything in this

house wouldn't *talk* at you," she said, in annoyance.

"Joe, you were carrying all the lunches," said Danny. "What did you do with them?"

"Oh, I put them away in a little cupboard in the kitchen," Joe said. "I'll get 'em."

The "cupboard" was a blue-enameled one beside the sink counter. Joe opened the door. A few wisps of blackened paper sailed gently out and sank to the floor. Instantly, another of the miniature vacuum-cleaner monsters shot out of its hole in one of the walls and sucked them up. But the children hardly noticed. They were staring in horror at the empty cupboard.

"It's an incinerator!" Irene gasped.

Joe moaned. "I'd give anything for an old-fashioned garbage pail. All my lovely peanut butter sandwiches, burned to a crisp."

"Not even a crisp," said Danny. "Okay, never mind. We're in a kitchen, aren't we? I know they have food in the freezer because I heard the Professor discussing the question of a cooking demonstration."

He went over to the built-in desk and sat down. A light went on, illuminating the console.

"This is the meal-planning unit," he said.

"You know, this whole kitchen is very interesting. First of all, when your household supplies get low, an indicator registers the fact and punch cards automatically list what's needed. A buzzer sounds, telling you it's time to order, and you just take the list and phone up the store."

"You'd think the list would take itself to the store," said Joe.

"I guess, some day, the ordering will be automatic," Danny replied. "Anyway, now suppose you want to prepare dinner. You look in your menu book to see what you have in the freezer."

He flipped open a leather-bound book on the desk, and ran his finger down the list of items inside.

"Roast chicken with mashed potatoes and peas. Okay for everybody?"

The others nodded.

"All right. You look at the code number— this one's D455-Ax. Now you push the proper buttons."

He did so. A blue light flashed on and from one of the machines at the far end of the kitchen there came a humming, and then a series of clicks.

"The food is being transferred from the freezer to the infrared oven," Danny said. "Now, I see that the cooking time listed in the program is two and a half minutes."

"Is that all?" Irene said, in surprise.

"Uh-huh. Because the infrared is so hot that it cooks the food right through in almost no time. So I punch the proper code number: two and five, and the heating setting, B-17."

From the polished steel oven came a buzz, and a red light flashed on in the console.

"We don't have to time it," said Danny. "I'll just signal the serving unit to stand by for two and a half minutes."

He turned a dial and pressed another button. A white cabinet rolled out into the center of the floor. It looked like their old friend, the Scuttler, except that a wide flat shelf stuck out of the front of it on two hinged arms, so that it seemed to be carrying a tray.

Joe, his mouth watering, was counting the seconds.

A bell chimed. The oven door flew open. The serving-scuttler glided to the oven. The shelf on the front of it moved forward and slid into the oven. It came out, bearing an aluminum foil platter on which was a whole roast chicken surrounded by a lake of green peas and a curling wave of mashed potato. The scuttler rolled to the table.

"Yum!" said Joe, hastily seating himself. "Over here, waiter."

Danny lifted the platter to the table. His face changed.

"Oh, jeepers!" he said. "I might have known."

Glumly, he raised a hand. With his knuckles, he rapped the roast chicken. It gave out a hollow sound.

"Plastic," he said.

"Naturally," said Irene. "They wouldn't cook real food over and over again for a demonstration. What idiots we are! I suppose it's all like that. Everything in the freezer must be plastic."

Joe threw back his head and uttered a whimpering howl, like a hungry wolf in the Siberian snow.

Emmet looked from one to the other. He leaned over and carefully licked the plastic chicken. His eyes grew rounder than ever. He touched the mashed potatoes with a stubby finger—they were plastic, of course, as well.

He caught hold of Joe's sleeve. His plump

face worked for a moment, and then, clearly and distinctly, he said, "Eat!"

The three older ones stared at him.

"Did—did you hear that?" Joe said.

"I did," said Danny. "He said 'Eat.' "

"Oh, boy," Joe said, in a low, tense voice. "Now we *know* the situation is serious."

11
The
Merry-go-Round

The sun was slanting in through the kitchen windows. The four children still sat at the long table. Danny had found a dusty bit of chocolate in one of his pockets and had given it to Emmet, who was nibbling it like a mouse. Irene had her chin propped on her palms. Joe was scribbling some verses on a scrap of paper.

Danny said, "There's one more possibility."

The others looked hopefully at him.

"You see," he said, "this whole house is a kind of robot. All the machines in it are parts of it, the way your arms and eyes are part of you."

Joe shuddered, "So we're trapped inside the stomach, like Jonah in the whale."

Danny snorted. "Oh, Joe, don't take everything so literally. Look there are all different kinds of machines in the house. Some of them are simple-minded, like the thermostats. They just do one easy job. Others, like the scuttlers, do more complicated jobs, find their way to you with dinner, or sweep up the floor. But there ought to be an overall control system which keeps everything running. A brain."

"Ah," said Irene, "you mean that it ought to work like a computer? A central information and command post, which tests the air for dust and temperature, keeps track of the electrical supply and the fuel oil, makes sure all the little machines are working properly—"

"Sure. And this brain might be programmed the way, let's say, an automated factory is programmed. It would have a printed circuit, or a punched card, or something, which tells the speeds at which things work and the way in which they operate."

Irene thoughtfully bit at a fingernail. "Not necessarily, Dan. Each machine in the house might follow its own directions. For instance, the scuttlers are probably all programmed individually."

"Okay. I know that. But if there's a basic program, and we could find it, maybe I could trace the door circuit and make it open. It's worth trying, isn't it?"

"I suppose so. It sounds dangerous. Where shall we start?"

"Open all the cupboards and closets first," Danny said. "Look for some kind of panel which might cover a box full of wires, or a printed diagram, or directions, or—anything."

"If you will excuse me," said Joe, "I will just go on with this poem. I wouldn't recognize a printed circuit diagram thingamajig if one came up and bit me."

Danny and Irene began a second tour of the house. They poked into every corner, opened every door or panel that would open. They had some surprises, as when Irene opened a very narrow door and a metal rack slid out and politely put an umbrella into her hand. They found several panels which were screwed into place, but when Danny got them open they turned out to be ordinary electrical junction boxes, or clusters of fuses.

At last, Danny said, "It looks like we're stuck. If there is a programming center, it must be outside. All I can think of now is wacky ideas like turning the radio set into a transmitter and calling for help, or sending up smoke signals."

"Smoke signals! Why not?" Irene said. "There's a fireplace in the living room."

"Gee, that's right." Danny snapped his fingers. "I remember your Uncle George saying at one of the meetings that there was no mechanical substitute for a nice, roaring fire."

They went to the hearth, which was of white brick with handsome brass andirons. Three birch logs were already laid across them.

"I'd better make sure they're real wood," Danny said, "and not some kind of plastic."

He tested them with his knife.

"They're wood, all right," he said. "We've got to find some kindling. We don't really have to send Indian signals. Just smoke pouring out of the chimney will attract attention outside."

It turned out to be a difficult matter to get any sort of kindling. Almost everything that was loose was made of metal or plastic. They took Joe's notebook away from him, in spite of his protests that he never went anywhere without it and wouldn't be able to write any more poetry. "Which do you want, poems or dinner?" Irene demanded. Danny gave up three pencil stubs. On an end table in the living room they found a copy of a gardening magazine which had been put there to make the room look lived-in. And that was all.

"It'll have to do," Danny said, tearing pages out of the notebook, while Irene did the same with the magazine.

They crumpled the paper tightly, put the pencil stubs on top of it, and laid two of the logs over all. Danny fished among the contents of his pockets and dug out his emergency camping kit: a tiny compass, a length of fishing line and a hook, and six kitchen matches which had been dipped in wax to keep them waterproof. With one of these precious matches, he carefully lighted a corner of the paper.

They all stood close, watching the flames leap up. The paper blazed brightly. The pencils caught, and the bark of one of the logs began to crackle. Then smoke began to fill the room.

"The damper!" coughed Joe. "You forgot to open the damper."

Flinching from the burning paper, Danny went as close to the fire as he could, searching for the rod which would open the chimney damper.

"Isn't any!" he choked. "It's a fake. Not a real chimney at all."

"We'll suffocate," Irene gasped. "And we can't even open a window."

All at once, it began to rain. At least, that was what it seemed like. From tiny openings in the ceiling, a fine spray of water poured. The automatic sprinkler system had begun to work, in response to the heat of the fire.

The children threw their arms over their heads, spluttering. Irene tried to shield Emmet as best she could, but he liked the shower and held his face up to it with his mouth wide open.

The water stopped as suddenly as it had started. The fire was nothing but a black puddle. The children were as soaked as if they had fallen into the sea. There was a whine as the air conditioning system went on, and the smoke vanished into vents in the walls. At the same time, strips of ultraviolet light went on in the ceiling, and a warm, dry breeze began to blow through the room. From several outlets, the vacuum-cleaner machines darted and began to rush back and forth across the rug in a vain attempt to clean up the water. Another scuttler, with towels hanging from a bar across its front, came scooting from the bathroom and made for Joe.

"Help!" Joe yelled.

He tried to get away from the scuttler, but it closed in on him. One of the cleaning machines ran between his feet. He jumped into the air to evade it, and when he had recovered his balance, backed up against the wall.

"Stop it!" he shouted. "How do you shut these things off?"

He scrabbled at the wall, looking for switches. His fingers closed around a knob, and in desperation he twisted it.

The house began to turn.

"No! The other way—!" cried Danny.

Joe gave the knob another twist. The house moved faster and faster, like a strange and stately kind of merry-go-round. Furniture went sliding away. The children were flung to the floor in a hopeless flurry of waving arms and legs.

12
The Right Key

Danny sprawled in a corner with a coffee table on top of him. He clutched at the floor and managed to pull himself to his hands and knees. Through the window he could see bushes reel past and it made his head spin worse than ever. There was something particularly dizzying in being inside a revolving house. It was like a nightmare: everything that should have been firm and solid was moving underfoot.

Gritting his teeth, he began to crawl towards the wall where the control knob was set. Joe was lying full length, trying to fight off one of the vacuum cleaners which persisted in its attempts to scoop him off the floor. Another of the miniature scuttlers was upside down nearby, its wheels still spinning busily. Irene was under a chair with two sofa cushions on top of her. She grimly hung on to Emmet and kept him from rolling about, although her own face was pale green.

Danny reached the wall. Here, because it was near the center of the house, the motion was not quite so bad. He was able to stand up. He grabbed the knob and turned it back, but not too abruptly for he didn't want to damage either the mechanism or anything in the rooms. As he turned it, the house slowed and finally came to a gentle halt.

Danny blew out a whistling breath, and mopped his face. "Everybody still alive?"

"I'm not sure," Joe said in a feeble voice. "I guess if I were alive this thing wouldn't be trying to eat me."

Dan tottered to his friend's side, pushed the little scuttler away, and helped Joe up. They both went to Irene's aid.

"Has the—ulp!—has the room stopped spinning?" she said, as they dragged her to her feet. "Oh, me. There was something awful about that. Worse than any merry-go-round I was ever on.''

"I know," said Danny, dusting Emmet off and standing him up. "It didn't go all that fast, but it was unsettling."

"Are you all right, Emmet dear?" Irene asked.

"Fun," Emmet said solemnly, having evidently decided to go on talking now that he had begun. Then, without any change of expression, he added, "Go home."

Danny laughed, and gave him a hug. "As soon as we can, Skipper."

Irene rubbed her eyes and ran her fingers through her hair to clear her mind. Then she said, "Dan, it's a funny thing, but in the middle of all that confusion and whirling I suddenly thought of something. I was thinking about the house going around too fast and about machines speeding up. And at the same time, I was thinking about the front door and saying, 'Oh, I wish you'd *open!*' sort of desperately to myself. I kept wishing that I could get the right key for it. And all at once, a memory popped into my head, of playing a phonograph record at the wrong speed."

She stopped, and looked at Danny with a

It was like a nightmare

slight frown. "Did you ever do that? Play a 33⅓ rpm record at 78 rpm's? You know what happens: the words not only happen much faster, they are all high-pitched and squeaky."

"Right!" said Dan. "I think I can guess what you're after."

"Yes. You said that the lock of the front door is keyed to a certain pitch of sound. That means, it has to take the word 'Open' spoken at a certain frequency, and match it against some sort of frequency-pattern inside and then the machinery will open the door. Well, we don't know how that's done, but suppose that when Joe banged against the wall he did something to the machinery so that now it will only respond to a higher pitch? Then the deep *voder* voice saying 'Open' won't fit any longer. It's the wrong frequency."

Danny beamed at her. "Irene, you're a whiz!" he said. "Sure, that could be it. Of course it's only a theory, but it's worth trying."

"But that's what I can't figure out," Irene said. "How are we going to get the *voder* voice to speak in a higher pitch—more and more cycles per second—until it matches what's needed?"

"We don't have to," Danny grinned.

"We've got a kind of skeleton key right here, one that ought to fit the door. Emmet!"

Hearing his name, Emmet looked up inquiringly.

"Professor Bullfinch was experimenting with him in just this way," Danny went on. "Emmet, my boy, you're going to get us out of here."

He caught the little one's hand and led him to the door. The others followed, breathless with excitement. Danny pulled up a small table and stood Emmet on it so that his face was level with the grill of the *voder* box.

"Okay, Emmet," he said. "You know how to talk, now. Say *Open*."

Emmet smiled. "Why?"

"Because," said Danny. "Just do it, Em. Say *Open*."

"Nope," said Emmet.

"Here," Joe said, "let me try. Emmet, chum. Emmet, little pal. This is Joe, Emmet. Say *Open* for Joe."

He bent close to the child. Emmet leaned towards him and dreamily licked his nose.

"Open," he said.

"That's it. Good! But now do it louder," said Joe.

"No—higher," Danny put in. "Way up

high. The way you did for Professor Bullfinch.
Sing, Emmet. Like this.''

He demonstrated, crying ''Open,'' in a fal-
setto voice that made him cough.

''Open,'' said Emmet, in a clear, shrill voice
like the squeal of a rusty hinge.

''Higher!'' said Irene. ''Ooooopen!'' She
made lifting motions with her hands.

''Open. Open. *Open!*'' Emmet's voice
soared up with each repetition until it was like
a bat's squeak. And then his voice vanished
altogether although his mouth kept on moving.

''— ——!'' he went.

There was a gentle click. The front door slid
aside as smoothly and sweetly as though it had
never given them any trouble.

They burst through it into the bright, hot
afternoon.

''Golly!'' Joe panted. ''I feel as though I've
been shut up indoors for a week.''

They turned all together and looked back at
the house.

Irene said, ''I sort of have the feeling it's
glad to get rid of us.''

Joe patted Emmet on the head.

''I've never been so glad to leave home before,'' he said. ''Now that we're free, the second thing I'm going to do is buy my little

buddy here the biggest hot dog he can eat."

"The second thing? Then what's the first thing you're going to do?" said Danny.

"Buy one for myself," Joe said, smugly.

13
A Fair Day

The opening of the Science and Industry Fair was impressive and exciting. The University band played, photographers' flashbulbs popped like summer lightning, the stand was crowded with celebrities, and Mrs. Dunn wore her new summer straw hat. The Governor of the State made a short speech (which most people felt was too long) and Dr. Sundergard, a lively man with a crew haircut and a tanned hawk-face, made a short, crackling speech (which most people felt was too short).

At the close of the ceremonies, Dr. Richards, on behalf of the faculty, invited the Governor to visit the Automatic House. The Millers, the Pearsons, Danny and his mother, and Professor Bullfinch were asked to join them, and Dr. Sundergard accompanied them although he had already seen the house in action. The young student guides were in their places and demonstrated everything; everything worked beautifully, and, as Irene whispered to Danny, the house behaved as though it knew it had distinguished guests.

"But I hear you youngsters had an interesting preview of the place," said Dr. Sundergard, when the compliments were over and they were all standing in the garden.

"It was interesting, all right," said Danny. "I don't know how they managed to get everything cleaned up and fixed up in time for today."

"It was quite a job," chuckled Professor Bullfinch. "At the same time, their escapade provided us with some stimulating material for our researches. I told you how they got the door open at last, didn't I?"

"Oh, yes," Dr. Sundergard said. "By checking system response to acoustical input at various frequencies. Fascinating what kids nowadays know. And are you all planning to become scientists when you grow up?'' he added, turning to the children.

''Irene and I are,'' said Danny. ''I don't know about Emmet, of course—''

''He's got the makings of a public speaker,'' said Uncle George, beaming fondly down at his son, who was holding one of his fingers. ''Since his exciting experience, he has done nothing but talk. I find myself occasionally yearning for the good old days when it was nothing but gibberish.''

''And what about you, Joe?'' asked Dr. Sundergard.

''Oh, I'm going to be a writer,'' Joe said. ''As a matter of fact. . . .''

''I'm sure I can guess,'' said Professor Bullfinch. ''I'll bet you've written a poem for the occasion.''

Joe nodded, modestly.

''Well, let's hear it,'' said Dr. Sundergard. ''Science and art should always be friends.''

Joe cleared his throat.

''The title of this poem,'' he said, ''is *The Ultraviolet Shines Bright in My Old Mechanical Home*. That has to be the title because I loved it but I couldn't fit it into the poem itself.''

Then he recited:

Wherever I wander, wherever I roam,
My heart's turning e'er to my automatic home.
My home on the range, it has up-to-date heating,
Electrical blankets, electric egg-beating;
I sit by the fire with the thermostat up,
On a quick-frozen dinner so blithely I sup;
My electronic armchair sings sweet lullaby
And we're quiet and snug, just my TV and I.
Not a creature is stirring, not even a mouse,
And the reason is this—it's a rodent-proof house.
Though I wander afar, where it's hot or it's
        breezy,
In my air-conditioned household the living is
        easy;
And although I may travel from Palm Beach to
        Nome,
I get letters from all the Old Robots at home.

Everyone applauded, and Mrs. Pearson drew herself up proudly and whispered to the Governor, *"My* son."

"Well, Bullfinch, I don't think we have to worry about the future of either art *or* science with these youngsters around," smiled Dr. Sundergard. He turned to Dr. Richards. "You must be pleased at the thought that these are your future scholars, sir."

Dr. Richards rubbed his chin. "I've known

young Dan for a good many years," he said, mildly. "Now, judging by our project here, which began as his idea, it looks as though we're going to have a hard time keeping ahead of him."

Dr. Sundergard chuckled. "And now, will you all join me in a tour of some of the other exhibits?" he said.

They turned to go. Irene's Aunt Joan, a plump, pretty woman, smiled at Mrs. Dunn. "We heard the whole story," she said. "How clever your son is!"

"And how fascinating that house is," said Mrs. Pearson.

Mrs. Dunn looked back at it. "Yes," she said, adjusting her new hat. "But you know, I feel a little about it the way some people feel about big cities. A marvelous place to visit, but I don't know that I'd want to live there."

Joe, Danny, and Irene had fallen a little way behind the grown-ups.

Joe began laughing. "Did you hear what Dr. Sundergard said?" he asked. "About how we got the door to open by checking system response and all the rest of it?"

"Sure," said Danny.

"Didn't it sound familiar to you?"

"Familiar? Why should it?"

Irene burst out laughing. "It did to me, Joe. Of course it's familiar."

"Where did you ever hear it before?" Danny asked, in bewilderment.

"Why, you ninny! It's exactly what you told the gate guard we were going to do," said Irene.

Danny blinked. Then he grinned. "That's right," he said. "I did say it."

"How did you know we were going to do it? That's what I want to know," Joe said.

Danny linked his arms in those of his friends.

"I didn't," he said. "But it proves you should never underestimate the power of a scientist."

And they began to run, to catch up with the others, so as not to miss any of the marvels of the fair.

ABOUT THE AUTHORS
AND ILLUSTRATOR

JAY WILLIAMS has written over twenty-five fiction and nonfiction books for children of all ages, in addition to coauthoring fifteen books about Danny Dunn. Mr. Williams was born in Buffalo, New York, and educated at the University of Pennsylvania, Columbia University, and the Art Students' League.

RAYMOND ABRASHKIN wrote and coproduced the very popular and successful "Little Fugitive," a film that won an award at the Venice Film Festival.

OWEN KAMPEN was born in Madison, Wisconsin. He attended the University of Wisconsin and for several years studied at the Art Students' League. During World War II, he was a B-24 pilot stationed in Italy. Mr. Kampen is a free-lance illustrator and portrait painter.